ANALOG COP

ANALOG COP

NATHANIEL JAMES

Analog Cop by Nathaniel James
Published by Publish My Book Online
www.publishmybook.online
© Nathaniel James

1st Edition 2019.
2nd Edition 2020.
ISBN: 978-1-925764-64-2 (print)
       978-1-925764-65-9 (epub)
       978-1-925764-66-6 (mobi)

Also available as an ebook from major ebook vendors

For Christine and Doris

"I guess a man is the only kind of varmint
sets his own trap, baits it, and then steps in it."
—John Steinbeck, Sweet Thursday

PART I

MILLER

CHAPTER 1

Westside, Baltimore

Lieutenant Kyle Copeland waited impatiently until the light on the camera-drone blinked off, signaling they were off the air. The poster-boy of the Baltimore Metropolitan Police Division had checked all the boxes. He'd turned on the charm for the reporter, downplayed the situation and, most importantly, warned people away from the Hippodrome Theatre and surrounding streets.

"Let's get out of here," said the reporter.

"Sorry, Ms. Mendel, we can't let you do that," Copeland said. "You leave cover, they'll fry you."

"But…"

"I'm sorry," said Copeland. "You wanted the exclusive."

Mendel flinched as a beam of green energy crackled against the blue light of the BMPD's force shields. Copeland followed her gaze, catching a glimpse of bright yellow and red as the sniper at the window ducked back, presumably not realizing the police couldn't return fire from behind the shields.

"Swell," she muttered.

Copeland flashed her a winning smile. "Don't worry. As long as you're behind the barrier, you'll be fine. In fact, this is the safest place around."

The reporter nodded, eyes wide.

Kyle walked away from the news crew. He opened the door of the closest van. "Wyatt, how are the generators holding?"

The balding technician swiveled around in his wheelchair and gave a thumbs up. "Shields are at hundred percent capacity, sir. We have twelve hours until the power cells need replacing."

"Plenty of time. Keep an eye on things. We're gonna make a move."

"Copy that."

Copeland closed the door and went over to where the rest of his team were huddled behind the other vans and squad cars, less for protection and more to conceal their numbers. Officer Sancha Alvarado, his right-hand woman, snapped a quick salute.

"Where's Sergeant Miller?" he asked.

"Haven't seen him, sir. I'm sure he's around somewhere."

"Fine," grunted Copeland. "Situation report?"

"Station confirms CK," Alvarado said. "All five of them."

"Those clowns? You gotta be kidding!"

"Red, green and yellow, it's them alright."

"I can't believe we're taking them seriously."

"They might be gimmicky, but their reckless shooting isn't."

"True. Have they responded to communication attempts yet?"

"Only with more shooting, sir. Mech-rifles, by the look of it."

"Terrific."

Precursors to the pulse rifle, mech rifles had been out-lawed due to their higher energy output, which increased the risk of crossfire casualties. Though more powerful, they were comparatively unwieldy and prone to overheating.

Copeland figured it was worth the risk.

"Plan, sir?" Alvarado asked.

He turned to the team.

"Listen up," he said. "It's confirmed; we are dealing with the City Kings. All negotiation attempts have been ignored, which leaves us no option but to engage. There are five targets, including two surgical enhanced—one with gills and the other with rapid tissue regeneration. Consult the visual files on your

DigiComms for ID. New intel says our targets are using illegal mech rifles, meaning our EDA suits may not withstand a direct hit. Make sure you shoot first. Stun, preferably. Lethal force if necessary. Understood?"

Everyone nodded. In recent years, special weapons and tactical training had become standard in the force, since there were no more paramilitary police units.

"Nine of you will form Alpha Team with me," Copeland continued. "We're going to make a frontal assault. Alvarado will head Bravo Team and provide cover fire."

"Understood, sir," said Alvarado.

Young, but sharp, the junior officer kept her cool under fire, with a steady shooting hand, and an acute awareness of her surroundings. Rumor had it she was in line for promotion to sergeant by the end of the year.

"And let Wyatt know we're going to use Big Boy," Copeland said.

"Sir?"

"You heard me."

"Yes, sir."

"We'll fire at the top floor, which should keep their heads down long enough to get inside. How quickly can we get Big Boy set up?"

"Shouldn't take longer than five minutes," answered Alvarado.

Copeland looked at his subordinates, scanning for a face which was conspicuously absent.

"Where the hell is Miller?" he asked, receiving only blank stares in response. He didn't particularly want the veteran cop there, but Captain Donovan had assigned him to his unit, thus Copeland was accountable for his whereabouts. "Somebody contact him and tell him to get his ass over here!"

"Sorry, sir," said Alvarado. "There's no signal from

his DigiComm. Either it's died on him or he's switched it off."

"Perfect." He dreaded the explanation he'd have to give to the captain.

"Keep your boots on, Lieutenant, I'm here."

He spun to see Sergeant Myles Miller walking up Eutaw Street toward them, looking more unkempt than usual. He wore his navy-blue mackintosh coat unbuttoned and his rumpled shirt looked as though he'd slept in it. His black tie hung haphazardly from his neck and his battered homburg was jammed tightly onto his head, the brim obscuring his eyes.

With distaste, Copeland noted the grass and mud stains on the knees of his slacks and caked onto his white joggers. His chin had not seen a razor in at least three days, if not longer.

"Where the hell have you been?"

Miller met the gaze of his superior. "It's the fifteenth."

"So?"

Alvarado looked at him, pointedly, and he suddenly remembered.

"Oh," replied Copeland, shamefaced. "Sorry. Just uh... gear up."

Miller nodded. He removed the mack, revealing his standard-issue blaster sidearm, then retrieved an EDA vest from the equipment van, rather than a full suit.

In the past, Copeland had questioned the wisdom of leaving so much of himself exposed. Miller would simply reply with: "If it's my turn to go, it's my turn to go." This concerned Captain Donovan, but the sergeant had steadfastly refused to attend counseling. "I have my own ways of coping," he'd say, though his teetotal reputation ruled out alcohol, and he showed none of the symptoms associated with the usage of Stimz or other recreational drugs.

"Where's your DigiComm, Sergeant?" He held up the device on his own wrist.

"It died," Miller said. Copeland suspected he was lying. The sergeant had a reputation for distrusting the "damn gizmos."

"I've got this, though," the sergeant continued. He produced an older radio handset with an earpiece and throat mic.

"How's that help?"

"The Digi-Comms are backward-compatible," Officer Alvarado said. "Wyatt can figure it out."

Copeland considered the grizzled sergeant. Average height, dark-brown skin, and the solid build of a pugilist; a contrast to the lieutenant's fair hair and complexion, tall, lean and clean-shaven. Even though he outranked Miller, he was still a few decades his junior. The sergeant was less a legend at the precinct and more of a fixture.

"Alright, Lieutenant, where do you want me?"

"You'll be Charlie Team," said Copeland. "Take up position around the back. Take Clarke, West and Nelson with you."

In other words, stay out of our way, old-timer

"Understood, sir."

"Good man," said Copeland. "Alvarado, how long will setting up Big Boy take with five pairs of hands?"

"Roughly nine minutes."

"Excellent. Alpha Team will assemble the blast-panels and get into position while Charlie Team circle around. I want everybody ready to go in ten minutes. Synchronize DigiComms."

The officers set their timers for ten minutes. Miller, using a battery-powered analog wristwatch, manipulated the dial, compensating for the extra moments it took him.

"Good luck, ladies and gentlemen. Let's move out."

Wasting no time, Alpha Team assembled a series of dispersive titanium and ceramic-carbonate alloy blast panels, scorched from previous use.

Meanwhile, Bravo Team hauled out Big Boy, an outmoded ionic particle cannon.

"Geez, this is a heavy bastard," one officer complained.

"Just be glad we only have the one," replied her companion.

Wyatt did a thorough check to make sure it was still intact and usable.

"This is gonna drain the hell out of our power-cells," he remarked.

"We've got permission to use the city's the power supply," Copeland said. "We're only allowed a ten-second burst, which gives us six seconds to get from here to the front door, plus another four to breach."

"Cool."

Under the watchful eye of Wyatt, a pair of officers opened a maintenance hatch in the street and ran fiberoptic cabling back to the cannon. Some might've argued that using an ex-military weapon that could down enemy airships was overkill, but Copeland believed in shock-and-awe tactics.

Ignoring the inquisitive news crew, the officers mounted the cannon to the roof of one of the vans and Wyatt powered it up. He aimed Big Boy up at the second floor.

"Alvarado, when the timer runs down, press that button and don't release until I tell you. I'd do it, but I need to turn the shields on again right away."

Alvarado nodded. "Fair enough."

"What about us?" asked the reporter.

"My advice?" said Copeland. "Get down and keep your eyes closed. This baby is gonna be bright."

●———————————●

Miller and his team positioned themselves by the rear stage door, the juniors briefing him as they went. He knew he'd been relegated to babysitting duty, but he didn't mind. Officers Denzel Clarke and Imogen West had only served for eighteen months and one year respectively, still qualifying as rookies. But they were both bright kids and Miller liked them, even if they did make him feel ancient in comparison.

Clarke was a sharpshooter and a family man. Miller had met his husband and their girls a few times before; nice family.

West was a natural enhanced with the ability to gain psychic impressions through physical contact. The public was still wary of enhanced people and an enhanced officer doubled the distrust, so Copeland probably wanted her well away from the cameras.

Miller didn't know enough about Bud Nelson—a new transfer—to pass judgment. The voices of the other group leaders came through his earpiece.

"Alpha Team in position."

"Bravo Team in position. Big Boy is primed."

"Charlie Team in position," Miller added, looking at his watch. He figured they had a good minute to go.

"We're doing this wrong," he said to nobody in particular.

"Sir?" asked Clarke.

"The City Kings may be gimmicky but they're unpredictable. We should be fast-roping onto the roof, hitting them from above."

"Lieutenant Copeland said it would take too long to get a helicopter here," said West.

Miller suspected there was a different reason. As far as cops went, he considered Copeland borderline competent but a glory hound. His decision to use the ionic particle cannon proved this. Ordinarily, that sort of showboating wouldn't fly. The BMPD, however, were in dire straits, both financially and when it came to public perception. Lieutenant Copeland was personable and telegenic; a face people trusted, and the BMPD tried to use him as much as they could. His leading this mission seemed little more than a sorely needed PR boost.

"Seven seconds," said Nelson, who'd been focusing on the DigiComm.

Five. Four. Three. Two. One.

Zero. Wyatt deactivated the force shield while Alvarado pressed down on the button. A harsh beam of dark-grey ionic energy lanced out from Big Boy and burst through the wall of the Hippodrome.

"Go, go, go!" barked Copeland.

Alpha Team sprinted out from behind cover, rushing up to the entrance. Alvarado watched Copeland slap the breaching charge onto the door and the crew moved aside as it detonated. Pulse rifles raised and ready, they followed him into the foyer. Emerging from the force shields, Bravo Team took up position behind the blast panels, aiming at the second floor, tinted visors protecting their eyes from the beam.

"*And release*," said Wyatt said over the DigiComms.

Inside the theatre, Chester "Chaos" Van Lewen listened to the commotion upstairs and smiled to himself. It was time to see if his new toy was worth the twenty-five thousand standard currency units he'd shelled out for it. This Mr. Smith character had better be on the level or there'd be hell to pay. Assuming the cops didn't gun them all down.

Showtime, he thought, smiling at his pun. He flicked a red switch on a small, gray box.

CHAPTER 2

A sensation of nausea flooded through Miller, causing the hairs to stand up on the back of his neck and his teeth to ache, then it was gone. It was a sensation he'd encountered once before, which did not bode well.

"Did anyone else feel that?" asked West.

"Yeah," said Clarke. "What was it?"

"My DigiComm's dead," Nelson said, confirming Miller's suspicions.

"So's mine," said West. "And my pulse rifle."

Clarke looked at his own weapons. "My sidearm too."

Nelson mashed the buttons on his wrist-mounted device, calling over and over again, panic mounting in his voice. "Wyatt, this is Charlie Team. We are experiencing technical difficulties, please acknowledge, over."

"Keep it together," said Miller.

West looked confused. "Sir, what's going on?"

"The bastards are using a theta wave."

"A what?"

"A theta wave," Clarke said. "It's like an electromagnetic pulse, except closer to a jamming signal than a single burst. Anything relying on complex electronics within a certain radius, including our weapons and DigiComms, is functionally dead."

"You're kidding!" said West.

"But that's fed tech!" Clarke said.

"That's right," said Miller. "And you're not supposed to know that."

Clarke went quiet.

Years before, Miller had participated in a highly secretive testing program as a favor to a friend, including a prototype theta wave transponder, and remembered the sensation he'd experienced when it activated. Clarke had probably read about it on one of the many conspiracy sites he was known to trawl. Perhaps these conspiracies weren't as leftfield as he'd first thought. Miller briefly wondered if he should invest in a tin-foil hat.

"Wait a minute," said Clarke. "The CK are using mech rifles!"

The BMPD, as with most law enforcement and other organizations in the country, used a computerized network system to regulate their gun usage, a response to outcry against accidental or unnecessary weapons discharge. Each weapon was satellite-linked, so no usage would go unaccounted for. Each pull of the trigger bounced a signal off one of the satellites to the computers at the station, authorizing the shot and logging the details for future reference within moments. No signal, no gun.

Mech rifles, on the other hand, relied on mechanical parts and had no such restrictions. The City Kings were armed and dangerous while the officers were now equipped with what amounted to InstaPlas toys.

"Alpha Team will be massacred," said West. "What do we do?"

"You can stay here if you want. I'm going in." Miller reached for the ancillary holster beneath his mack. "These creeps want old-fashioned, I'll give them archaic."

While it wasn't uncommon for police officers to carry a smaller, secondary weapon, a ballistic firearm was exceedingly rare. Miller held a Heckler & Koch Ultimate Combat Pistol that had once belonged to his father. Sleek, compact; a work of art. And no electric parts to be affected.

The third junior officer's eyes widened for a different reason. Ballistic weapons weren't officially illegal, but without any means of regulation, they were frowned upon.

Miller noticed this right away. "Report me if you want but stay the hell out of my way."

He kicked in the door and stepped back, UCP at the ready. Seeing nobody, he walked in, Clarke and West following close behind.

Nelson didn't follow.

Inside, Alpha Team had fanned out, advancing cautiously through the lobby. From the corner of his eye, Lieutenant Copeland made out Officer Blankes moving his head slightly to the left and adjusting his grip on his pulse rifle.

"Keep it tight, Blankes," the lieutenant said quietly over his DigiComm. "Eyes front, use your peripherals."

"Yes, sir."

"See anything yet?"

"Negative... wait, I—"

A brief wave of nausea washed over Copeland, then he realized his DigiComm had gone quiet.

"You wanna repeat that, Blankes?" No response came. "Blankes?"

The junior officer stood not five yards away; Copeland could see his lips moving, though no sound came through the DigiComm earpiece.

Glancing up, he saw the King known as Colby slowly walking toward Blankes, mech rifle hanging lazily from one hand.

"Police, don't move!" ordered the junior officer, taking aim at the CK.

Colby only smirked at him.

"You've been warned!" Blankes squeezed the trigger for a stun shot, and nothing happened. Confused, he looked down at the weapon in his hand.

Copeland noticed his own gun had gone dark too. "Blankes, get down!"

His warning came too late, as Colby casually raised his gun and fired upon Blankes.

BMPD Energy Dispersive Armor suits were designed to protect against blaster fire, but mech rifles had ten times the output of modern lasers that EDA suits were designed to negate.

Instead of being harmlessly redirected, the green bolt punched through Blankes' armor *and* his body.

Copeland watched in horror as Blankes shuddered once, then dropped to the ground, dead.

Colby shifted his aim and the lieutenant threw himself aside as the CK fired again. The officer behind him wasn't fast enough and took the full brunt of the shot directly through her visor. Copeland cursed and scrabbled around behind the bar, narrowly avoiding a third and fourth blast.

In the space of five seconds, two of his people had been killed. At any second Colby would circle around the bar and fry him too.

•————————•

The backstage corridors were quiet. There were no lights, but Clarke and West lit the way for Miller with a pair of Hyginium emergency road flares.

Miller saw another beam of light attached to the barrel of a mech-rifle held by one of the Kings. He recognized the dark shades and pointy goatee of Brick from the visual files Nelson had shown him.

Brick raised his rifle and Miller dove forward. In almost perfect unison, Clarke and West pressed themselves up against the walls as Brick fired, the bolt passing between them.

From his position on the ground, Miller put three 4.6 caliber bullets into the CK, two in the chest, one in the throat. Taken by surprise, Brick fell with a harsh gurgling sound, dead before he hit the ground.

"Ouch!" said Clarke, holding his ears. "I didn't realize how loud those things are."

"Sorry!" yelled Miller, whose ears also rang.

The sergeant nudged Brick with his foot, UCP aimed at his unmoving form.

"I don't think he's getting up," West said, a little too loudly.

"Never hurts to check." Miller examined the bullet wounds. Unlike modern firearms, which had a digital readout indicating the percentage of energy left in the cartridge, his pistol required him to count each bullet. He'd fired three shots, leaving him with sixteen rounds, plus one in the chamber. So long as he kept his aim steady, he had enough ammo for the remaining Kings.

Removing a glove, West placed her hand on the fallen man's neck, closing her eyes in concentration.

"Anything?" Miller asked.

"A few echoes, but nothing useful."

"Alright, let's keep going then."

Clarke, the better shot of the other two, picked up the fallen gun and a spare cartridge. Not wanting to give their position away by further shouting, Miller signaled for them to follow him into the backstage area.

Downstairs, Copeland lay on the floor, desperately pressing himself into the corner in an effort not to be noticed. Colby strolled around the bar, spotting him instantly.

Grinning, he placed the muzzle of the gun against Copeland's chest, then pulled his helmet off. Exposed, Copeland didn't move.

"Well, well. If it ain't the hero cop."

Copeland didn't say anything.

"Don't worry, pal. I'll make it quick," Colby said.

Copeland froze as the King pulled the trigger.

Nothing happened.

Copeland reacted first, bringing up his own weapon and striking him under the chin. Kicking him away, the lieutenant scrambled to his feet, then hit Colby with a flying tackle.

——•——————•——

Backstage, Charlie Team split, Clarke striking out on his own, with West lighting the way for Miller. He held up a hand when he heard footsteps approaching and the junior officer hid.

A gaunt, lanky individual the files identified as Goliath came into view.

"BMPD, don't move!" Miller ordered, aiming his pistol.

Goliath ignored him, raising his mech rifle. But when Miller tried to fire the UCP, the gun did no more than click.

Jammed!

Nothing happened when Goliath pulled the trigger on his gun either. The mech rifle had overheated. The City King threw down his gun and charged.

Miller tossed the UCP directly at the King, who batted it away. But it allowed him time to land a straight left to the punk's jaw.

A boxer in his youth, Miller knew how to throw a punch. Goliath's head rocked back with the impact, but he didn't falter. He followed up with a second and third punch to the abdominals before the CK kicked out wildly.

It was a lucky strike, connecting with Miller's right knee, weakened by a previous injury. He gasped as pain exploded through his leg, allowing Goliath to knock him off his feet.

Pressing a knee to his chest, the City King grabbed him by the throat and squeezed. Miller couldn't call out. He thrashed, but Goliath applied more weight, pinning him in place.

Behind the King, he glimpsed West desperately trying to unjam the UCP. Something dropped to the floor, then a shot rang out.

In the inexperienced hands of West, the shot went wild, the kickback almost snapping her wrist.

Goliath rounded on the officer, rage in his eyes. Miller took advantage of the distraction to reach for the Buck 110 Folding Knife concealed in the sheath around his ankle. He plunged the blade into his opponent's foot.

Goliath roared in pain. He bent down to wrench the offending blade from his foot as Miller, gasping for air, tried to crawl out of reach. He'd barely gone a few feet when a hand seized him by the ankle and began dragging him back.

Something skittered along the ground and he blindly reached for it.

The pistol.

Goliath lifted a foot to stamp down on his face. Wasting no time in aiming, Miller snapped off four shots. Two missed completely, the third slammed into Goliath's abdomen and the other tore through his ear, sending him spinning to the ground.

Miller allowed himself to go limp on the floor as he tried to catch his breath. His throat hurt like hell, but he was alive. A dozen rounds remained in his gun.

"Um, Sarge?"

Miller lifted his head to see West pointing at Goliath, who was getting to his feet, bullet wounds closing over before their eyes.

Oh yeah, he thought. *Rapid tissue regeneration.*

CHAPTER 3

The acrid stench of propellant stung Miller's nostrils as he fired again and again while moving backward. Goliath flinched with every hit but continued at a steady pace toward him.

Having ordered West to run ahead, he stayed behind to slow the King. Each wound healed within moments, pushing out the bullet as it closed.

Miller had a single round left and wasn't thrilled at the prospect of going hand-to-hand with him again. He backed onto the stage, UCP leveled at Goliath. He couldn't outrun the younger, fitter enhanced with his dodgy knee. If he focused, he might get in a lucky shot between the eyes and scramble his circuits long enough to get away.

"Sarge!" called Clarke from somewhere. "Don't move!"

Trusting his junior, he stayed still, keeping his gun trained on Goliath, who broke into a run.

"Clarke!" His finger squeezed tighter against the trigger. "Make it snappy!"

Then Goliath vanished.

Miller was so surprised he didn't have time to shoot.

For a few moments, nothing. Then the faint crunch of a body impacting solid ground came from below. He looked down at a gaping hole in the stage and realized he was looking down at a trapdoor.

A grinning Clarke came to his side. "Pretty cool, huh?"

"How'd you know about that?"

"Remmy and I brought the girls to see *Potterpalooza* here a couple of weeks ago," Clarke said. "They took us backstage to see how it all works,"

"Isn't that dangerous for the performers?"

"Nah, they're all trained in how to fall properly and there's usually a crash-mat in place. By the sounds of it, they remove it between productions."

"Get him cuffed. I'll meet up with West."

Clarke nodded and went downstairs.

One bullet and at least three hostiles remaining. Miller didn't know how many officers were left standing and there was still the theta wave to neutralize.

"Yo, Mister Policeman!"

Miller turned to see Officer West standing in one of the aisles, face to face with Chaos Van Lewen. He held a blade to her throat.

"Lose the gun before I fillet this pretty young thing, yeah?"

Miller didn't budge. "Don't move, West. I can nail him from here."

But he knew she had him right where she wanted him.

In a blur of movement, she lashed out and the base of her palm connected with Van Lewen's chin, causing his head to snap backward, and he fell to the ground.

To the casual observer, she'd laid out a man with a good two feet and about a hundred pounds on her with one hit, but Miller knew she'd used another facet of her enhancement to turn Van Lewen's own memories against him to the point of sensory overload.

"Psychic feedback?" he asked.

West nodded, hunching over, hands on her knees, breathing heavily.

Holstering his gun, Miller went to her. "You okay?"

"I'll be fine."

After a few more moments, West placed her hand on the back of the criminal's head. "Seventh row."

Miller snapped a pair of electro-lock cuffs on Van Lewen, then went to investigate. Under the middle seat, he found a small, gunmetal gray box with a single red switch, glowing on top. He flicked off the switch, removed its power cells, then pocketed the device.

He turned to West. "Let's finish this."

———————

Things had taken another bad turn for Lieutenant Copeland. Colby had managed to struggle back to his feet, bringing Copeland with him. The officer noticed a yellowish tinge to his eyes; a dead giveaway of Stimz use.

No wonder he's stronger, he thought.

He didn't notice the body of Blankes until he stumbled over it. Colby cackled, going for the kill, when somebody called out. "Hey, Polly Parrot, over here!"

Colby turned and fired at Alvarado, who ducked behind a pillar, giving Copeland time to get away.

Copeland didn't know how or why she was there, but now Colby was gunning for her. "Hey, chucklehead!" he called, trying to draw attention from her. "You can't shoot us all. Why don't you give up and let us take you in?"

"That's where you're wrong, pig," growled Colby. "I can shoot every one of you, again and again, and love every second of it!"

"I'd rather be a pig than a dairy product," he laughed, relying on the wit which had so often landed him in trouble at the academy. "You're only threatening to the lactose intolerant."

"At least I can back it up with a working gun," Colby sneered. "You're just shooting blanks. No wait, that was me."

Copeland stopped laughing.

"Come in all teams," came a voice over the DigiComms. *"This is Wyatt. All systems are back online!"*

"Thanks, Wyatt," he said. "Just what I wanted to hear."

The lieutenant stepped out, drawing his sidearm, engaging the ID pad with his thumb and switching off the stun function. Colby brought up his rifle, but Copeland was quicker, tagging him half a dozen times in quick succession, even after the other man dropped.

"Warned you." He spat on the body.

"Stone cold, sir," said Alvarado.

"What happened to the guy upstairs?"

"I pitched a flashbang up at him and he dropped out of sight. I dunno what happened after that.."

"Fine."

The man in question—Monster—was unconscious when they found him. After reeling back from the stun grenade, he had struck head and was now out cold.

"Make sure our people are seen to first," ordered Copeland.

Miller's team showed up carrying Van Lewen between them. They accounted for Brick and Goliath.

The accompanying officers waited for the healing process to finish then slapped on a pair of power suppressing restraints before he could wake up.

With two dead, two sedated and one going into intensive care, the City Kings had lost the conflict. The BMPD had still taken several fatalities; too many in Copeland's books. The division had barely enough officers as it was, and now he'd lost a fifth of his team. He felt sick. There was no doubt their deaths rested squarely on his shoulders.

The realization came with a difficulty catching his breath. He walked away, vaguely aware of Sergeant Miller talking to him but he sounded distant. Unreal.

Taking off his DigiComm and removing the power cells, Copeland slipped out a side door.

CHAPTER 4

Miller sighed.

Since nobody knew where Lieutenant Copeland had disappeared to, it was up to him as the senior officer to take responsibility for the impending media storm. It was the part of the job he hated most.

Several more reporters arrived on the scene, digital pads and camera-drones at the ready, and he fielded rapid-fire questions about what had happened. He carefully curated his replies, wary of implicating the division any further. Their reputation was precarious enough as it was. At least no civilians had been injured in the conflict.

He was grateful to Clarke and West, standing nearby for moral support.

Inevitably, the questions moved away from the situation at hand.

"Sergeant, can you comment on the reports regarding the division's funding cuts?" asked one reporter. "Are we looking at the dissolution of the police service in Baltimore?"

"Unfortunately, I'm not qualified to comment on the future of the division, or its financial position."

"Sergeant Miller, do you think the division's current situation is in part due to aftershock in light of the Metro Mutilator case?"

Miller felt his jaw clench and curled the fingers of his left hand into a fist. "No more questions."

Ignoring their protests and flanked by the junior officers, he stepped back into the theatre, where he submitted to an examination by the paramedics. Aside from some bruising around his chin and neck, he checked out fine, so he rang Captain Donovan.

"It's done."

"Casualties?"

"Four of ours are dead, several wounded."

A heavy sigh on the other end. *"And the Kings?"*

"Two dead, the rest subdued."

"Civilians?"

"None reported."

"Well, that's something."

"And Copeland's disappeared."

"What? He was supposed to keep an eye on you!"

"I'm sure he'll turn up. I'll give a full report tomorrow."

"Alright. Look after yourself, Myles."

He supervised as the hard-light police bands were set up around the theatre, assigned perimeter detail, then headed to his G50 Phantom, ignoring the reporters.

His job was done.

———————

Miller found himself growing tired more frequently these days; a side effect of growing older, exacerbated by his job. He wanted to go home and sleep but that would be fruitless with the adrenaline still coursing through his body. Instead, he drove to the park.

Druid Hill Park had been one of Marion's favorite spots. He stopped at the small stall near the entrance, which had been faithfully manned by Dopinder Parikh for as long as he could remember.

"Good afternoon, Sergeant," the old man said. "The usual for you?"

"Yes please, Dopinder." *Straight, black and piping hot, like me,* he used to joke, always making Marion roll her eyes and try not to smile.

"I saw the Hippodrome on the news," said Parikh, preparing the order. "I take it you had something to do with that?"

"Something."

He took the hint. "Well, enjoy your coffee, Sergeant." He handed over the paper cup.

Miller prepared to pay, but the barista waved it away. "Please. Today, it's on the house."

He nodded his thanks, then followed the footpath, enjoying the cool, early evening air. He sat on a bench overlooking Druid Lake as he drank.

Every month on the fifteenth, Miller visited his wife's grave at Green Mount Cemetery. It was the fifth anniversary of her death. Kidney failure. He'd laid a bunch of snapdragons—Marion's favorite—on her grave, heedless of the mud caused by the previous night's rain.

When his old phone chimed, he ignored the incoming call and switched it off. He didn't cry. Not out of a need for machismo—he'd been inconsolable the first week. He just no longer had the capacity.

A few wet leaves covered the headstone, which he wiped off with a handkerchief so the inscription could be read again—a quote from Samuel Beckett. Something about the melancholy and dark humor in his work had held a morbid fascination for Sergeant Marion Miller during their thirteen-year marriage. Reluctantly at first, he'd allowed her to drag him to various underground, amateur and community productions of his work—some in French—and even a main stage production of *Godot* at the Hippodrome. Absurdism wasn't his bag but seeing her eyes light up and her rapt expression as she watched had endeared the Irish playwright to him.

I can't go on. I'll go on.

The quote perfectly encapsulated Miller's attitude in the following years. His days were filled with bouts of dysphoria and loneliness, interspersed with small satisfaction from life's simple pleasures. Many an hour he'd spent locked away in his room with his music, as in his teenage years.

He'd become withdrawn and soft-spoken yet managed to maintain a level of effectiveness as a police officer. Still respecting the rules, he had his own way of doing things.

Captain Donovan, a close friend of the Millers, had shown great tolerance toward his quirks. The routine helped, as did mentoring the younger officers. He and Marion had always wanted kids, but with their involvement on the force, time had eluded them until it was too late. The juniors were the closest he'd ever come.

He enjoyed the company of Clarke and West, though balked at socializing outside work. Sometimes he needed to be by himself. Of course, unless something was done, there might no longer be a BMPD to speak of.

For another hour he sat watching the lake, then tossed his coffee cup in the trash and drove back to his block of flats.

His landlady, Mrs. Hansen, stood in the doorway and waved him inside the building. "Thank goodness you're here, Myles. I'm locked out again!"

She showed him the security door which had shuttered over the front of her flat "Ever since I got this damn thing, I've had nothing but trouble. Do you think you could use that override code thing?"

She was referring to the public override code given to members of emergency services, programmed into nearly every door in the city.

"Sure, Mrs. Hansen. Where's the control panel?"

"Inside."

"I need to access the controls to enter the code."

"Oh. I thought you had remote access?"

"Not me."

Miller inspected the DuroSteel plating. He could just make out a brand name and serial engraving. *Knox Security Solutions.* They were commonplace throughout the city, touted as extremely safe and extremely affordable.

"I think I can get it open. I'll have to dig into the wall, though."

"I don't care about that. I just want to get inside before my dinner burns!"

Reaching down, Miller took his Buck knife from its sheath and opened it. "Whereabouts are the controls located on the wall?"

Mrs. Hansen pointed.

Miller dug the point of his knife into the plaster. Applying pressure, he sliced a rough hole in the wall, pulling a chunk of plasterboard away and carefully placing it on the floor next to Mrs. Hansen.

He reached a hand in and felt around until he touched the back of the console. A little more probing and he found the indentation and opened the access port. He handed his flashlight to Mrs. Hansen. "A little light, please?"

She switched it on and shone the beam into the hole in the wall. "What are you doing?" she asked, curious.

"My father used to install these," Miller replied, as he re-jigged the wires inside. "I used to watch him. Sometimes he'd let me help."

He heard a faint beep and the security door slid open.

"There you go," he said. "Faulty wiring. KSS have really let their standards slip."

"Myles, you are my hero!" Mrs. Hansen proclaimed.

"No problem. You might want to cover that hole up and call them back out in the morning. If Leroy's still there, ask for him."

"Thank you so much! I'd say that's worth a week's rent right there."

"Happy to help," Miller said and went up to his own apartment.

He fed his Siamese fighting fish, Spartacus II, and retired to the spare room. Shedding his hat, mack and shoes, he climbed into the single bed. He touched his middle three fingers to Marion's photograph on the bedside table, turned out the lights with the control pad, and fell asleep.

●————————●

Pulsing techno music blared in his ear, jolting him awake. For a few disorienting moments, Miller didn't know what was going on until he remembered letting West change the call-tone on his phone.

It was quarter past two in the morning. He'd slept for eight hours straight, but it still didn't feel like enough, and he ached from his fight at the Hippodrome.

Groggily, he answered. "Hello?"

"Myles? It's me."

Captain Donovan.

Miller worked himself up into a sitting position. "What's up, Fiona?"

"I need you at the station. A few visitors want to talk with you."

"Late for visitors, isn't it?"

"Tell me about it," she groaned. *"One flew in from D.C. especially."*

Miller mentally cursed. "You're kidding me. A fed?"

"Afraid so."

He didn't like her tone.

"Just get down here as soon as possible, please."

"Yes, ma'am," he replied, ending the call.

He took a sharp breath in, letting it out with an elongated huff as he switched the lights back on. In ten minutes, he had showered, brushed his teeth, and was out the door in a fresh shirt and pants.

His stomach grumbled as he drove, reminding him that he hadn't eaten since early the day before. He stopped at an all-night Greasy McGee's drive-thru and bought a lab-grown tuna melt bagel and a cup of coffee.

At twenty to three, he arrived at the First Precinct. He contemplated going back home instead, but Donovan had requested him. If she was in trouble with the FBI, he would back her up.

Steeling himself, he ascended the steps and went in.

The graveyard crew was well into their shift. Lieutenant Heeth—a natural enhanced with acute night vision—waved to him. "Little early, aren't you, Miller?" she asked with a grin he did his best to return.

"I'm here to see Donovan."

"Sure, go on in." She gestured with her mug. "I swear she hasn't gone home for three nights. Gouveia's cranky because she won't let him into the office."

Miller wouldn't have been surprised if that was the case. He thanked Heeth.

He found Donovan seated behind her desk looking worn and weary. Her clothes were rumpled and the gray streaks in her unkempt hair seemed more pronounced. She'd been overdoing it again, and the presence of the others in the room clearly didn't help any.

Miller recognized the first man straight away—Police Chief George Hesseman, who didn't look much better. Ranking just below deputy commissioner, he was generally liked, even if his years behind a desk had left him a little out-of-touch. Formerly a fine police officer in his own right, his ambition led him to rise through the ranks, thrusting him prominently into the public eye, meaning he also dealt with city officials and blowhard bureaucrats. It was sad, in a way, to see such a bold man walking on eggshells for the good of the division's image.

The fed—black suit, neat left-part, red-rimmed eyes—he didn't know.

"Sergeant Miller," said the captain. "You know Chief Hesseman, and this is Agent Gregory Nichols, FBI."

Both men nodded in acknowledgment as Miller sat on the chair opposite the captain. "I'm all ears."

Donovan pressed a button behind her desk, causing her computer monitor to grow translucent, revealing news footage, and flipped the screen for him to examine. The text beneath read *Hippodrome Havoc,* and the images mainly comprised of the gaping hole in the second level of the theatre from Big Boy.

"This hack job piece was up barely an hour after the incident," she explained, "by the same reporter who interviewed Lieutenant Copeland. After Officer Alvarado saved her life when the force shields went down no less. The general gist is that the BMPD's presence only served to escalate matters and they're calling for a public investigation into our operations."

Miller nodded. This was nothing new.

"Our PR people are trying to mitigate the damage, but there are dozens more snippets and articles, spreading like wildfire."

"Commissioner Steuben is obviously concerned. The last thing we need right now is more scrutiny," Chief Hesseman said. "We need to generate some goodwill and fast. To that end, Agent Nichols here has a proposal."

Miller glanced at Hesseman and noticed that his immaculately clipped mustache sat a little crooked; the shave of a time-poor man.

"Sergeant," began Nichols. "First of all, thank you for the return of the theta-wave transponder." He pointed to the carry case on the desk. "Our tech boys will be glad to get it back. However, I'm primarily here to talk about your involvement in the Crane case."

Miller tensed at the name. Known publicly as the Metro Mutilator, Phineas Crane was a serial killer who exclusively targeted BMPD officers.

"There's nothing to discuss. He was a criminal, and we captured him."

"Don't give me that," Nichols said. "Twelve officers went in, and only you came out alive. How come?"

"Dumb luck."

Since the state of Maryland had long ago abolished the death penalty, Crane had been placed in a private maximum security facility. The thought of that freak still drawing breath turned his stomach. "What's your interest in Crane?"

"There is a copycat killer on the loose in D.C.," said Agent Nichols. "Six of our agents have been murdered in a manner almost identical to Crane's M.O. We have a few seconds' worth of surveillance footage showing somebody in a powered exosuit attacking one of our men."

"The FBI thinks there's a connection," said Hesseman.

"Everything I know about Crane you can find in my reports," said Miller. "I'm sure Captain Donovan provided you access to those."

"We need more than that," replied Nichols. "We want you to talk to Crane and seek his input."

Miller shook his head. "I don't want anything to do with that murdering psychopath."

"Crane can't be bought, threatened or intimidated," continued Nichols.

"He's resistant to truth serums, and even if the use of enhanced mind readers for interrogation purposes were legal, we'd still have no way to verify their findings."

"And that's where I come in?"

"That's right," said Hesseman. "As the man who brought him in, you may be the only one he considers worth talking to."

"That's a big maybe."

"It is," said Nichols. "But we are getting desperate. The president himself is becoming concerned."

"No," said Miller. "Just let him rot."

"Please, Sergeant. The commissioner is breathing down my neck because the feds are breathing down his," said Hesseman. "He believes a successful joint venture with the FBI could really help us."

"This is your duty as an American citizen," Nichols said. "In any case, we only want you to talk to him, see if he can offer any insights regarding our mystery killer."

"What do you say?" asked Hesseman.

Every instinct of Miller's yelled for him to refuse. But then he thought of Marion. She had always encouraged him to help people.

He thought of Donovan. The captain had common sense, empathy and integrity; a rare combination for someone at or above her rank. She spoke bluntly when called for and didn't believe in ass-kissing, which greatly diminished her popularity among the senior ranks.

Steuben could have contacted Miller directly instead of involving the chief and the captain. If he refused, the commissioner's simpering cronies would go after them. He couldn't allow it; they were two of the few senior officers who knew what they were doing.

"Alright, I'll do it."

Nichols gave him a translucent digital pad—wafer-thin, yet extremely durable, with a recording device to capture any nuggets of wisdom Crane might share.

"One more thing, Miller," the chief said. "We need to keep this quiet and contained. If word gets out that we're working with a serial killer, it'll reflect badly on the division which could jeopardize our efforts to get more funding from the board next week."

"They still talking about privatizing us, huh?"

"It worked for Michigan and Georgia. They figure it might work for us."

Miller stood, jamming on his homburg. "And here I thought we were an institution."

———•———

A few hours later, Miller sat on the hood of his G50 Phantom in the Charles Centre One visitor's parking lot. Given what he was about to undergo, a little liquid courage would not have been remiss. As a teetotaler, however, he had to make do with his sixth coffee in the last twelve hours. His doctor would flip if she found out how much caffeine he was consuming—especially at his age—but she'd do the same in his position.

The center had been converted into a maximum-security facility by an organization called SyndiCorp. Since the BMPD couldn't afford to maintain such a facility, Crane had been placed into their custody instead. It wasn't exactly ideal, but that was how things had to be.

The sergeant looked at his watch—five past nine, give or take a few minutes. He should have called in Clarke or West for moral support but didn't see much sense dragging them into it.

His phone chimed twice. He looked and saw a message from the captain.

```
You're better than him. Don't let him
make you think otherwise.
```

Miller wasn't so sure.

Now or never, he thought.

Taking his sidearm from the glovebox, he holstered it, locked the car, then headed inside, dropping his cup in a trash can on the way.

A senior officer greeted him in the lobby. "Sergeant Miller, I'm Allondra Conway." She offered her hand. "Chief Hesseman told me to expect you."

"Sorry if I'm throwing your routine out of whack, ma'am."

"Not much of a routine—keep 'em in their cages and feed 'em twice a day."

"How many are being held here?"

"Five at the moment but what we lack in quantity, we make up for in quality."

"Where's Crane?"

"Right down the bottom, in our most secure cell. Believe it or not, he's not the worst offender we have."

"I'd hate to see who is."

Conway laughed humorlessly, turned and marched briskly down the corridor. Miller practically had to jog to catch up with her.

"You probably know the supervising officer. A former Sergeant Collins."

Ezecki Collins had graduated from Baltimore Police Academy alongside Miller. The two never had gotten along; Collins was the kind to shoot first and *maybe* ask questions if the thought occurred to him afterward. He'd left the force a few years previously. Apparently, the lure of better pay had convinced him to go corporate.

"Frankly, Sergeant, I am wholeheartedly against this idea," said Conway, snapping Miller back to reality. "Working with this individual won't end well."

"Agreed, ma'am." He was glad somebody could see sense.

Conway stopped in front of an elevator and turned back to him. "I'd be lying if I said I didn't want to just blast his brains out. Unfortunately, neither of us are in a position to defy the police commissioner or the FBI."

"Not if we want any kind of career in this city, ma'am."

"Hell, maybe it'd be worth it. You lost good officers to that sick bastard."

"Nobody knows better than I do."

Conway nodded her understanding. "Let's get this over with." She pressed her hand to the biometric scanner. The elevator doors slid open and they stepped inside. She punched a sequence into the control panel, the doors closed, and they descended into the bowels of the facility.

CHAPTER 5

Stepping out of the elevator, Miller noticed a temperature drop immediately and was grateful for his mackintosh. It had been the last gift from Marion, specially imported from the UK.

Watching him adjust the coat, Conway smirked. "We keep it colder down here on purpose." She shrugged on a jacket herself. "Makes our guests more docile."

Walking down the corridor, they came to another set of doors—Conway opened them via retinal scanner—through which lay a room lit by the glow of a dozen computers. Two rugged-up techs stood as Conway entered. Their name-tags read Haggler and Redding.

"Good morning, sir," Redding said with a snappy salute, causing Haggler to roll her eyes.

"Good morning." Conway didn't bother to return the salute. "Where's Collins?"

"Out getting schooled in chess again," said Haggler.

"Call him in," ordered Conway. "And prep Sergeant Miller to see Crane."

Haggler turned back to the computers, while Redding approached Miller. "No weapons or comm devices allowed, Sergeant."

Miller complied, removing the blaster and UCP handgun, then unbuckling the knifesheath from around his leg, placing them in the plastic tray the techie provided, along with his phone and digital pad.

Redding placed the tray on the desk behind him and picked up a screening wand. Scanning revealed no additional weapons, electronics or metals aside from his watch, and Redding gave Conway a thumbs up.

"Before you go in, Sarge, a few house rules," Redding said. "Most of them are pretty self-explanatory, but we're obligated to inform you, regardless."

"Okay."

"Don't approach within five feet of the containment cell; the prohibited area is marked out in red along the platform," recited the tech. "Keep one hand on the railing at all times. You will be monitored by six cameras and four armed guards. Should any of the guards issue an order, it must be followed. If an escape attempt should occur, the entire facility will immediately go into lockdown. You may be escorted out if possible or forcibly detained if necessary."

Miller nodded after every point, concentrating instead on calming himself. Despite having every reason to be agitated, he knew if he went in angry, Crane would easily get under his skin, he wouldn't get any useful information and this whole excursion would be for nothing. He tried to recall the breathing techniques Officer West had taught him.

After fiddling with the digital pad Agent Nichols had given Miller, Haggler handed it back. "Your device has short-range transmission, so it's okay," she explained. "You can send information to us or to the sister device in the cell but nobody outside the facility."

"If Crane decides to cooperate, you can transmit a copy of the data files Hesseman sent me," said Conway. "But I wouldn't be too hopeful."

Miller found the recording function and turned it on, slipping the pad into the inner pocket of his mack. "Worth a shot."

Through the surveillance room door, the air grew colder yet again. The artificial breeze blowing along his neck disquieted Miller and he tugged up his collar. Two guards stood on either side of the door, rigid and imposing, watching as he stepped out on to the strip-lit gangway.

It wasn't until he saw the man coming from the opposite direction that he remembered to grab hold of the railing, opening his body more to his unseen observers.

The man drew closer, and the familiar scent of cheap cologne assailed his nose. "Miller," he said.

"Hello, Collins."

Aside from a little salt and pepper in his crew cut, Ezecki Collins hadn't changed much since the academy. He stood six feet, five inches tall, with a physique once straight out of a Charles Atlas history vid, now with a little more padding, causing his jacket to look several sizes too small. A pair of dark aviator sunglasses sat crooked on the pockmarked face of a brawler, whose expressions alternated between smirking and scowling. Both were equally unpleasant, and today was further marred.

"Your nose is bleeding," said Miller.

Collins touched a hand to his nose. As he brought it away and saw the spots of blood, his scowl intensified. "Dammit!"

"Are you alright?"

"Guess I've been overdoing it." He took a tissue from his back pocket and pressed it to his face. "I'm fine."

Collins continued to the surveillance room without even shoulder-checking Miller as he passed. That surprised him. Had he matured since the academy after all? Then again, Collins never admitted to anything remotely resembling weakness. Miller suspected the dark glasses hid a pair of eyes with a distinct yellow tinge.

The chamber was enormous. Miller spotted the light of the fire safety system faintly glowing from the ceiling some twenty-five yards away. Presumably, the distance below was similar, if not greater. Above, he could feel the gaze of two guards on a hidden observation deck. He kept his pace steady, making no sudden movements until he came to the red line.

A chessboard, mounted on a stand, was set up along the edge; an invitation to play a game.

Miller ignored the board, turning his attention to the cell itself. A perfect cube, it hung at the end of the walkway suspended by six high-tensile steel cables. Two sets of LED floodlights, attached to either side of the chamber, illuminated the cell. Apart from a solid metal floor and rear wall, it was comprised of reinforced, triple-layered DuroGlass panes, allowing him to see inside.

The cell's interior was sparsely furnished—a thin, springless mattress and a hardened polymer-plastic toilet in one corner, with a single tap sink attached. Two small vents in the rear wall, covered by grilles, provided air circulation. As Conway had explained, this doubled as a security measure. If the occupant should touch the DuroGlass, the pressure-sensitive surfaces would simultaneously trigger an alarm and cause the vents to fill the cell with a sedative gas. *Pity it's not something lethal,* he thought darkly.

Stock still in the middle of the cell stood Phineas Crane, his back toward Miller.

"Crane," he called.

Turning around, Crane saw the sergeant and smiled, displaying uncannily straight teeth. Though seemingly genuine, the effect was disconcerting. Physically, he'd changed little from when Miller had last seen him—tall and pale with the ectomorphic build of a professional decathlete and angular facial features. Light gleamed off his shaven head, as it did the metal bracer on his right arm. The dark-red prison uniform was immaculate, without so much as a crease, save for the left sleeve, folded back over the stump where his forearm had once been.

Crane reached up and touched the digital pad embedded in the glass of the cell, activating a speaker function.

"Sergeant Miller," he said, in the silky English baritone that had charmed and disarmed many an unsuspecting American. Miller had always suspected it was an act, but if it was, Crane's performance never faltered.

"What an unexpected surprise. Nobody told me *you* would be visiting."

"Wasn't planning to."

Crane smiled again. "I'm afraid, in my current state, the hospitality I can provide you is limited." He gestured around his sparse cell. "Unless I could interest you in a game of chess? You'd have to move all the pieces, of course."

"Sorry, I prefer checkers."

Crane sighed. "Unsurprising, but disappointing. Then again, you never struck me as the social type."

Keen cobalt eyes scrutinized him until Crane arched an eyebrow in realization. "The FBI sent you." There was a hint of amusement in his voice. "Gambling I may hold you in high enough regard to provide assistance to you. They must be desperate to catch my impersonator."

Miller wasn't surprised he had put two and two together. "I don't wanna be here, but the feds are throwing their weight around. The last thing they want is a Metro Mutilator of their own."

Crane flinched. "I always despised that melodramatic moniker. Is it so much to expect the press to use my proper name?"

"Guess the media doesn't care for humanizing monsters," Miller said, coolly.

Crane looked taken aback. "Touché, Sergeant. That's something I always admired about you; you never sugar-coat. What you lack in elegance, you make up for in dogged determination and 'straight-shooting,' as you Yankees say."

"Great, the validation of a psychopath," said Miller. "What I always wanted."

"Come now, Sergeant." Crane affected a hurt tone. "Surely there's no need for namecalling. I think I shall help you after all."

"Just like that?" Miller asked skeptically. "After holding out so long?"

"Merely a question of the right person asking."

"Me?"

"Of course." His eyes glittered. "Out of all the BMPD, it was you who bested me in the end, through sheer tenacity and fortitude."

"Right place, right time."

"Don't undersell yourself, Sergeant. You caught me fair and square, and you have a strength of character so rare within your organization. You've earned my respect."

"Cut the crap," growled Miller. "Are you helping or not?"

"You know your trouble, Sergeant? You can't take a compliment," tutted Crane. "Very well, show me what you have."

With slow, deliberate movements, Miller reached into his mackintosh and, with some difficulty, produced the digital pad. With his left hand still firmly grasping the railing, he managed to send the files to the device in the cell.

"Excellent," said Crane. "Please allow me a few minutes to peruse."

He didn't see he had much of a choice, and patiently stood by as the prisoner studied the files. He found himself glancing at his watch as the minutes ticked by, wishing he could be anywhere else, with anybody else.

"Interesting," Crane said at last. "There's footage of the imposter in action. He's skilled, though lacks panache. His style is flashy and gratuitous."

"Do you have anything?"

"I believe I have a lead for you, which I will gladly share on the proviso that I accompany you in the investigation."

Miller wasn't sure if he'd heard correctly. "Excuse me?"

"I want to come with you."

"You want to go free?"

"Not entirely. I would be under your supervision, naturally," Crane clarified. "Presumably with whatever security measures Conway determines."

"Oh, I get it," said Miller. "This is British humor us dumb Americans don't get, right?"

"I'm quite serious, Sergeant. I'm curious to see you in action, and the view from in here has grown terribly dull. There are only so many times I can play Minesweeper or Solitaire on this infernal device or attempt to teach that oaf Collins to play a decent game of chess. I haven't read a book in months. It's time for a change of scenery."

Miller stared at the prisoner. The plasma scarring on his left hand from their last encounter began to itch. With the current medical technology, such a superficial blemish could be easily rectified, but he kept it as a reminder that twelve went in alive, one came out. "No way. Let yourself out."

"I consider myself fairly capable, Sergeant, but I'm no Houdini."

"You could always drown yourself." He pointed at the toilet in the cell. "Save us all some grief."

"Harsh, though not unwarranted," Crane conceded.

"Help us out, and I'll make sure you get all the books your withered little heart desires. Hell, I'll even learn the rules of chess and come in every week to play. Best and final offer."

"No need to be facetious, Sergeant. And it's not good enough. I get out or you get nothing.

"Fine. I'll ask."

"Good. Until you do, you and I have nothing further to say."

Crane placed his hand on the glass panel in front of him. Immediately, sirens sounded and lights flashed as blue clouds of sedative gas poured into the cell. He stepped backward, disappearing into the swirling fog.

Miller rolled his eyes. "*Now* who's melodramatic?"

As he turned, he saw Conway running up with both armed guards and the two techs. "What the hell did you do?"

"He's sulking," said Miller.

"Did you get anything out of him?"

"Not yet."

Conway turned to Haggler. "Take the sergeant to his vehicle, then come straight back. Find Collins. We need a full system reset."

"Yes sir," said Haggler. "This way, Sarge."

The techie led Miller back up the elevator and out to the parking lot, which was now enclosed on all sides by DuroSteel shutters.

"We're in lockdown," Haggler explained. "You're stuck here until we sort things out. Try not to set off any more alarms."

She turned and headed back to the lobby before he could respond. Leaning against the side of his car, Miller mentally played back his interaction with Crane. There had to be some clue in what he'd been told but he could only focus on the sickeningly superior grin the Mutilator had given as he'd vanished. After all he'd done, he had the gall to request freedom?

The more he fixated on it, the more he began to burn, until his left hand began to ache.

Looking down, he saw he'd bloodied his knuckles punching the concrete pillar next to the Phantom. *Gotta cut down on the coffee,* he thought, noting how his pulse raced. Breathing deeply, he calmed himself before fishing through the glovebox for the first aid kit. Luckily, the damage was no more serious than a few scrapes; easily treated.

Sitting in the driver's seat, he gripped the steering wheel, staring ahead, waiting for the shutters to open. When they did, he gunned the engine and tore out of the complex.

As he drove, he called Captain Donovan via the dashphone. He reached her message bank. "Fiona? Myles. Crane will only talk if we release him."

He hesitated.

"Under any other circumstances, I wouldn't even think about it. But if Hesseman is right, and this is the win we need, we might just have to go for it."

CHAPTER 6

While Miller waited for further instructions, he chose to visit his last living relative.

Jazz Wiley was Marion's younger sister and the one person who had come close to loving her as much as he had. She was a typical troubled sibling, constantly living in the shadow of the "good daughter" and running with the wrong crowd.

The image of Jazz breaking down during his eulogy at the funeral, awkwardly comforted by whichever new man she was with at the time, was indelibly burned into his consciousness.

As a posthumous promise to his wife, Miller did his best to keep an eye on her as Marion once had. Some days he saw the chipper, irreverent young woman he'd first met, other times, the aggressively obstinate juvenile. Mostly, she looked numb; a blank slate.

She didn't answer her phone, nor was she at her apartment. He checked her regular hangouts and eventually learned her whereabouts from a reluctant friend of hers. She was with a man over in Sandtown, a part of Baltimore which had proven resistant to change for longer than Miller's fifty-five years.

A young man with matted blond hair and an oily complexion answered the door. "What do you want?"

"I'm looking for Jazz Wiley," said Miller. "Is she in?"

Blondie regarded him with suspicion. "Who's she to you?"

"My sister-in-law. I want to see her."

"She doesn't want to see you."

With a frustrated grunt, Miller flashed his ID. It was archaic in this day and age, but it was still effective as a status symbol. "You can cooperate, or you can enjoy the next few years in a cozy little containment cell. Your call."

Blondie moved to the side, scowling at him as he passed, but did nothing other than close the door behind him.

"Good choice."

The ramshackle apartment was a far cry from the modest yet clean one the Millers had rented for Jazz. A figure wearing a hoodie huddled on the couch, staring blankly at the switched-off television.

"Jazz?"

No response.

He moved forward, aware of Blondie pacing back and forth behind him. He only cared about the woman on the couch. Bunched up hoodie sleeves revealed pale, bony arms, wrapped tightly around her knees.

Miller tried again. "Hello?" The figure shifted, saying nothing.

"I wanted to make sure you're okay," he continued. "You need anything? Money? Groceries? Doctor's appointment?"

She shook her head.

"You gonna talk to me?"

Another shrug, then a vague voice replied, "Yeah… I guess."

Something in her tone roused his suspicions. "Jazz, turn around. Let me see your face."

"Hey man, leave her alone," chimed in Blondie.

"Stay out of this," he growled without looking back. "Turn around, Jazz."

She shifted again, making to get up from the couch, so Miller clamped a hand down on her shoulder. "Jazz!"

She turned slowly, avoiding looking directly at him. He reached up and pushed back the hood.

Tangled, silvery hair framed her narrow face and hadn't been washed in weeks. Her skin was blotchy and her nose was an angry red. Her vacant eyes held a tinge of yellow.

He groaned. "For crying out loud, Jazz, you're using again?"

Glaring, she shook off his grip. "Guess I am."

Miller pressed a fist to his forehead, squeezing his eyes shut. He couldn't believe it yet wasn't altogether surprised. "You were doing so well. Seven months Stimz-free!"

"Yeah," sneered Jazz. "I was real proud of myself, so I thought I'd celebrate."

"What happened to your hexothil tablets?"

"They kept me awake at night." She jabbed a thumb toward the other man. "Modsy traded 'em in for something a little more fun."

What the hell kind of name is Modsy? thought Miller. "We agreed we were going to kick this."

"So I didn't live up to my side of the bargain. Big deal."

"It *is* a big deal, Jazz. I made a promise to look after you."

"And how's that working out for you, big guy? I'm a grown woman, Miller. What I do is my own damn business, not yours."

"That's not gonna fly with me, Jazz." He grabbed her by the arm. "Get up, get your coat. You're coming with me."

"Hey, pig!"

He turned and bright white light exploded in front of him. A blizzard of spots swirled and danced before his eyes and he cursed, blinking furiously.

"Modsy, don't!" called Jazz.

A fuzzy human outline entered his field of vision, too tall to be Jazz. Miller reflexively swung out with his right elbow, clipping the side of Modsy's head. As Modsy reeled, Miller drew the blaster and thumbed the ID pad. In the same instant, he remembered a shot would be tracked and didn't want to deal with the questions bound to follow.

Not wanting to give the Department of Internal Affairs anything to hold against him, he swung out with the butt of the gun instead, catching Modsy in the chin, knocking him down.

"What the hell, Miller?"

"Light tap," he replied, eyes finally clearing. "He's fine."

"He has a weak heart," Jazz said. "You could have killed him!"

"If he'd juiced up before I arrived, that could have killed him too. Or worse, you."

"Why do you keep following me?" she asked. "My sister is dead, so, as far as I'm concerned, we aren't related anymore."

"You need help, Jazz."

"I'm fine!" she yelled. "And even if I wasn't, why would I ever want help from a has-been cop?"

He didn't answer. Ignoring the wailing, writhing form of Modsy, he pulled the sleeve of his mack over his hand. He took the two Stimz pens from the coffee table. He turned to his sister-in-law, who was staring balefully back at him. "Where's the rest?"

"That's all we had."

"Jazz…"

"They were provisional," she insisted. "Modsy is on thin ice with Rakeem."

"Is Rakeem your dealer?"

The look on her face said she had revealed too much and she fell quiet. A quick search of the apartment revealed no more, and Miller took a gamble that she was telling the truth.

He walked into the tiny kitchen with the Stimz pens, dropped them into the incinerator unit, and they combusted with a dull *whump*. Satisfied, he returned to the living room where Jazz knelt next to Modsy as he groaned and stirred.

She glared up at him. "Now what? You gonna arrest us?"

"What good would that do? No. I'm going to ask you to go to the clinic on Charles Street and get yourself back into the rehab program. Take this idiot too. I'll look after the bill when you finish, and we'll work together to make it stick this time."

"Why don't you take me?"

"I don't have time, Jazz."

"Forget it, then. If you can't be assed taking me, why should I even go?"

She had a point. He didn't care. "Don't make this difficult!" he shouted. "I'm losing my patience with you!"

"Go on then, Miller, leave. Like you left Marion."

He felt his knees weaken. Those few words hit harder than any enhanced.

Jazz went on the offensive. "Deny it all you want, Miller— at the end of the day, my sister spent her last days without you. You weren't at her side, and it destroyed her. And don't you dare tell me not to talk about her. I knew her longer than you, I knew her better than you, and I loved her more. You might have married her, but I was there for her. Whenever she needed to talk, who did she turn to? It sure as hell wasn't you."

He couldn't move, couldn't speak, couldn't look away. He boiled inside, but something held him in place.

She's right.

Neither Miller nor Marion had known anything was wrong until Marion had reached the fourth stage of chronic kidney disease. Even then, they'd associated most of the symptoms—weight loss, muscle cramps, poor appetite—to the stress of their job. By the time she'd been diagnosed and begun treatment, it'd progressed to stage five.

Soon, Marion was on dialysis. Miller would have donated one of his kidneys in a heartbeat, but they hadn't been compatible, and while Jazz's were, her use of drugs rendered her own kidneys unsuitable for a transplant. Marion was put on a list, but she had had a long wait ahead of her.

Miller put in hours and hours of overtime so they could have a better chance with private health care, often coming home too exhausted to do anything but sleep. He had been working on the other side of town when she'd taken a sudden turn for the worse. By the time he'd arrived at the hospital, she was gone. It still haunted him.

Jazz showed the fresh puncture mark on her arm from the Stimz pen. "This is your fault too. Yesterday hit me like a ton of bricks. I couldn't be by myself. I tried to call, but you never answered."

Miller vaguely recalled ignoring an incoming call. "So you hang out with this junkie instead?"

"At least he answered. Don't keep pretending to care about me and don't pretend you cared about Marion, either. You only loved her when it suited you, otherwise, you shut her out, too. And when she couldn't take it anymore, you abandoned her."

Miller had had enough. Reaching down, he hauled a sorry-looking Modsy to his feet and frog-marched him toward the door.

"I'll be back on Monday, Jazz," he said as he went. "If I find out you haven't been to rehab, I'll drag you in myself."

No response. Glancing back, he saw she'd moved back to her spot on the couch. Forcing Modsy out the door, he closed it behind them.

"Ow!" complained Modsy. "Cut it out!"

Sick of his voice, Miller slammed him up against the corridor wall. He was a little disappointed the man didn't seem concussed.

"You're lucky I don't have time to arrest you." His voice was calm, but the grip on his collar told Modsy otherwise. "But the two of you are done. If I find out you're so much as *thinking* about her, your buddy Rakeem will find you out cold in an alleyway with a three hundred standard transfer token and the phone number of a DEA official in your pocket. I'm sure you don't need me to tell you what that'd do to your rep or your life expectancy. Am I clear?"

Modsy nodded frantically.

Miller dropped the junkie, who scrambled away on all fours. He left the apartment with a bitter taste in his mouth and the same sense of nausea he'd experienced exactly five years and one day ago.

CHAPTER 7

Cursing under his breath, Miller stepped into the lobby of Charles Centre One. He couldn't believe he was doing this. But Commissioner Steuben thought it was a great P.R. boost, promoting cooperation between law enforcement, and had insisted they go ahead.

Allondra Conway met him at the door, looking no more thrilled.

"Your bosses agreed to this harebrained scheme too?" said Miller.

She nodded. "Just reset everything too."

"Sorry."

"Chain of command." She sighed. "What can you do?"

He had a few ideas he wasn't proud of.

The elevator ride passed in silence. Reaching the bottom floor, Conway made a detour into the armory to retrieve a pulse rifle. "I *pray* he tries escaping," she said, inserting the energy cartridge. "Then again, accidents *do* happen."

"If it does, you know I'll have to accidentally arrest you."

Conway sighed. "Yeah, yeah. Let's get this over with, Sergeant."

In the chamber, the guards stood ready, pulse rifles trained on the figure in the cell. Miller counted three more than last time. Collins was nowhere to be seen.

Haggler and Redding met them at the gangway, looking nervous. "Ready when you are, ma'am," Haggler said.

"Where's Collins?" asked Conway. They shrugged. "Never mind, I'll talk to him later. Let's go."

Two guards led the way onto the platform, Conway and Miller followed behind, with Haggler and Redding bringing up the rear, lugging a carry case.

The guards took up positions on the red platform, either side of the cube. Drawing closer, Miller spied Crane seated in a full lotus position, eyes closed in meditation.

Unfazed by the cold, he'd removed his uniform top, revealing scarring, bruises and burn marks from an electroshock weapon. Some of the injuries couldn't have been more than an hour old, and dried blood ringed his nose.

Miller pulled Conway aside. "What the hell happened to him?"

"Collins got a little carried away restraining him," Conway replied.

"Does he get carried away a lot?"

"Only when Crane beats him at chess. Which *is* a lot, come to think of it."

"Ma'am, I mean no disrespect, but are you out of your mind? How could you allow this?"

Conway scoffed. "You think he doesn't deserve it, after what he's done? He killed people and you're worried about civil liberties?"

Miller balled his left hand into a fist then released it. "Phineas Crane is the biggest threat the BMPD have encountered in years and you have him sealed away like a spider in a glass. You know what he's capable of and you want to aggravate him?"

Conway faltered. "He isn't our problem anymore." She turned to the cell. "Crane! Wake up!"

Crane opened his eyes, stood and slipped on his shirt with surprising deftness, having only one arm.

"Ms. Conway, Sergeant Miller," he said. "And to what do I owe this little gathering? Are we having a tea party?"

"Shut up, Crane," said Conway. "You're getting your wish."

"Splendid." He stepped back and held his arm alongside his body.

"Tell Cooke to hit it," ordered Conway.

Haggler activated her comm device and relayed the instructions to a third technician hidden in another room. A low thrumming filled the chamber as a series of electromagnets built into the rear wall of the cell powered up. The magnetic field took hold of the metallic bracer on Crane's arm and held it against the wall. His legs bore similar restraints, and Crane was effectively stuck to the back of his cell. Luckily, the equipment used by the guards was comprised of non-ferrous materials and were unaffected. Unfortunately for Miller, it made his old watch go haywire. He made a mental note to have it looked at.

An automated winch pulled away the ceiling and DuroGlass walls of the cell. With the alarm system deactivated, Haggler and Redding were able to move into the red zone and the remainder of the cell.

Redding set down the carry case and opened the lid, taking out a rudimentary prosthetic arm. With some difficulty, he attached the prosthesis to Crane's left stump, sealing it on with a liquid adhesive. It was plastic, without articulated joints. It wouldn't give him much more in the way of mobility but was crucial to the next step.

"De-mag one," said Conway.

The sound of the electromagnets lessened as one of them deactivated, allowing Haggler to slip a second, thicker bracer over the prosthesis without getting stuck to the wall.

"De-mag two and lock the cuffs."

A second electromagnet released Crane's arm, only for both forearms to snap together across each other as Redding remotely activated the magnet housed in the left bracer. Cautiously, Haggler moved forward and tugged at the manacles, which did not budge.

"Shackles secured, ma'am," she reported.

"Good," said Conway, then addressed Crane. "You are to follow each and every instruction Miller issues to you. I hereby authorize whatever application of force he deems necessary should you fail to comply. I also authorize lethal force should you attempt to escape or harm him in any way. Am I understood?"

"Perfectly," replied Crane.

"Haggler, tell Cooke to de-mag three and four."

The techie relayed the order and the electromagnets quietened. Everybody watched to see what Crane would do.

Moments—lapsing into ages—passed, though he did no more than clear his throat, causing Redding to jump.

"Well?" he said eventually. "Shall we get on with it?"

At gunpoint, Crane stepped out onto the walkway, arms above his head. Once he was ten paces across, the rest followed. On the far side, the guards watched their approach, pulse rifles unwavering.

It wasn't until they entered the observation room that they encountered a problem in the form of Ezecki Collins.

"I'm going too," he said, powering toward the group.

"No," said Conway. "I need you here."

"Crane is my responsibility. I'm not letting him walk free. He needs to be watched."

"Miller can handle it."

"No offense, Miller," said Collins. "You were lucky last time, but you won't have a squad of meat shields to hide behind now."

Incensed, Miller nevertheless managed to keep his cool. Collins had never been one to think before he spoke.

"You're staying!" Conway barked. "That's an order, Collins!"

Collins opened his hand, revealing a data drive. "This says otherwise."

Frowning, Conway took the drive and hooked it into the closest computer. Opening it, she found a message from none other than the Governor of Maryland. It decreed the prisoner known as Phineas Crane was the personal responsibility of Ezecki Collins, SyndiCorp Security, regardless of the venue. "How the hell did you get this?"

"All that matters is that it's authentic. Verify it if you don't believe me."

Conway pressed a button on the console. "Cooke, you there?"

"*Yes, ma'am!*" answered a woman's voice.

"I'm sending you a file. I need a verification."

"*Right away, ma'am.*"

They waited as Cooke compared the verification sequence to the one supplied by the governor's office.

"*It's a match,*" she reported, sending through the results. "*He's on the level.*"

"Damn," growled Conway. "This is trouble I *don't* need." Miller frowned.

"Will you still assist if Collins joins us?" he asked Crane.

"Of course. The more the merrier! It'll give Collins plenty of opportunities to redeem himself on the chessboard."

Miller saw Collins' eye twitch.

"Sorry, Miller," said Conway. "You're relegated to third wheel."

"It's okay. I'm getting used to having no choice lately."

Haggler handed Collins a handheld device and the carry case. "That's the mag control for the cuffs. There's a spare prosthetic in the case."

"Gotcha."

Conway took Collins aside for a quick word, then shook hands with both men. "Good luck, fellas. And Crane, don't make me regret this."

"I wouldn't dream of it," he replied with a smile, as they stepped back into the elevator.

———•———

Collins and Crane exited the lift at the staff parking bay, while Miller continued to the visitors' parking lot. Taking what he needed from the Phantom, he locked it, then walked outside, where Collins met him with a containment van.

As he jumped into the passenger seat, he glimpsed Crane, tucked away in the back, bracers stuck to the magnetized rail, separated by five inches of strengthened DuroGlass.

"Where to?" asked Collins.

"Central Precinct." Miller read a new message from Donovan. "Chief Hesseman and the fed want to see me."

"Us," said Collins.

Miller brooded as they drove.

"We need more people. Crane can dismantle a twelve-person squad; two old guys aren't gonna be a problem for him."

"First of all, speak for yourself," Collins retorted. "Secondly, relax; he's not so tough without his suit and those cuffs aren't coming off for anything. Thirdly, if all else fails, there's still the implant."

"Implant?"

When Collins grinned, it was devoid of warmth, and he had a glint in his eye that hinted at a secret. "Yeah, Crane was under anesthetic for his last medical, so Conway organized for an extra procedure."

"What kind of procedure?"

"She had him injected with these microcapsules. Harmless by themselves, but trigger the right ultrasonic signal, they disintegrate and release a slow-acting toxin into the bloodstream. Kill the bastard in about fifteen minutes."

"How the hell did she manage that?" Miller asked.

Collins tapped the side of his nose. "Strictly off the books."

Miller glanced back at Crane again, who gave no indication of having heard.

Collins saw and sniggered. "Don't worry, the screen is soundproof."

"Are you kidding?"

"Nope, I was there. Even tailed the doc for a few weeks to make sure he wouldn't blab. Unfortunately, only Conway can activate the capsules."

"Where did she even get those?"

"Beats me." He shrugged. "Black market, probably."

"Geez…"

Poisonous micro-capsules. It was something out of those campy old spy movies, something a villain bent on world domination would use. Sure, it couldn't happen to a nicer guy, but it seemed uncomfortably underhanded. Then again, Collins could be messing with him.

"I have to check in with Conway every five hours or she'll assume something is up and activate the signal," said Collins.

"*Every* five hours?"

"Morning, noon and night, which means we'll have to take shifts watching Crane."

"Terrific."

Collins pulled up outside the First Precinct and took an electroshock shotgun from the compartment beneath his seat. He covered Crane as Miller de-magged the rail.

"Out you get," ordered Collins.

"Come now, Collins," said Crane. "Where are your manners?"

"You can come out or I stun your ass and drag you out."

"Take it easy," said Miller, wary of antagonizing their prisoner. "Please, Mr. Crane, we want this to be as smooth and painless as possible."

Crane smiled again. It unnerved Miller no less. "Of course, Sergeant. And thank you for your civility."
"Sure."

CHAPTER 8

The precinct was abuzz with activity when the trio entered. Everybody carried on as though there were no looming threat of unemployment. Officers bustled about carrying mountains of backlogged paperwork to be digitized, transferring perps or taking statements from John and Jane Q Citizen. Nobody noticed the incarcerated serial killer walking in their midst.

Almost nobody.

Clarke and West were waiting by Miller's desk and spotted them right away. As they came closer, Clarke saw Crane. With a curse, he drew his sidearm and focused it on the prisoner, West seconds behind him.

"Whoa, easy!" Miller raised a hand. "Hold your fire but keep him covered."

As he spoke, he noticed Crane visibly start at the sight of Officer West. He wasn't the first to react in such a way; without her tactical armor and helmet on, the rookie's bald head and hairless features were in full view.

"It's rude to stare," Miller said.

"A-hem… yes. My apologies."

"Sir, is this who I think it is?" asked Officer Clarke.

"Unfortunately, yes."

"Why is he here?"

"It's complicated," Miller said. More people were taking notice and hands crept toward blasters. "Trust me, he wouldn't be here if there were any other option."

"What do you want us to do?" asked West.

"I need to speak with Donovan. Keep an eye on Crane until I get back."

"Happy to," said Clarke.

"If he tries anything, shock his ass," said Miller, then quietly added to Clarke, "The same goes for Mr. Collins."

The junior officer nodded, and Miller went to the captain's office.

———•———

Officer West watched Phineas Crane.

If he was perturbed being surrounded by police officers, he gave no indication. "Any chance of a cup of tea?" he asked, earning only frosty stares in response. "Hmm, pity. It's been absolutely ages since I last had one. Then again, it's probably for the best; police station beverages are notoriously sub-par."

No reaction.

"Now, you, my dear, are quite fascinating," Crane said to West. "I've seen your condition before. Alopecia, isn't it?"

"Ignore him," said Clarke.

"It's alright," replied West. "No harm in being polite. You're right. Universalis, to be exact."

"Well, correct me if I'm wrong, but they developed a cure thirteen years ago, did they not?"

"That's right."

"Then why live with it when there's a cure readily available? Surely you attract a lot of unwanted staring?"

"I'm bald, not disfigured," West calmly replied. "Alopecia doesn't define who I am. It's a part of me and not a part I'm ashamed of."

She glanced over at Clarke, who grinned at her response.

Even Crane looked satisfied with her reply. "A commendable attitude. Public perception is overrated."

"Alright, enough chit-chat," cut in Collins, gesturing to the chair next to Clarke with his gun. "Take a seat, Crane."

Crane sat, saying nothing more, still staring at Officer West.

———•———

Miller sat across from the captain for the second time in twelve hours as he explained the situation with Collins. If Donovan had been exhausted before, she looked frazzled now. The chief looked anxious, and Agent Nichols looked pleased with himself.

"We have Crane," said Miller. "Satisfied?"

"Oh yes," said Nichols.

Miller frowned. Were the FBI genuinely desperate to catch the copycat or was Nichols merely after a promotion? Either way, he was playing with fire. "What's the plan?"

"I figure the bodies are as good a place to start as any," said Nichols. "We'll fly to D.C. first and examine a few of the victims. Should give Crane some ideas."

"Whatever you say."

"Agent Nichols," said Donovan. "Sergeant Miller is one of my best officers. What assurance can you give me that he'll be safe?"

"If you've followed correct prisoner transport protocols, he will be perfectly safe."

Miller wasn't reassured by that.

"With respect, sir, protocols fail," said Donovan. "I'd be a lot happier if they had more people. Perhaps a few more agents?"

Nichols shook his head. "We're stretched too thin at the moment. We can't spare anyone."

"In that case, sir, I'll contact the D.C. chief of police and let her know about Crane. If things go south, they can provide backup or set a perimeter around the city."

"That's probably a good idea," Chief Hesseman said. "I'll contact her myself. Alright by you, Agent Nichols?"

"Fine, but *only* as a precaution. I don't want to complicate things."

Or share credit, thought Miller.

They were interrupted by furious knocking. Donovan pressed the button behind her desk to open the door and Officer Nelson rushed in. "Ma'am? We have a situation in the bullpen."

Fearing the worst, Miller bolted from the room.

The floor was not littered with cop corpses. About a dozen additional sidearms were now pointed at a sitting Crane. A couple of officers had even brought out a few pulse rifles from the armory. Collins wore a look of amusement on his face.

"Everybody stand down, now!" bellowed the chief. "That is an order!"

Everybody complied, though all eyes remained warily on the prisoner.

Hesseman rounded on Miller. "Sergeant, what the hell were you thinking, bringing a cop killer into a building full of cops?"

"I didn't want to take any chances leaving him alone with Collins." Truthfully, he'd also worried about the questionable stability of the former officer. "They were bound to find out."

"He's right," said Donovan. "Now you can talk to everyone at once and prevent potential vigilante action."

Hesseman sighed. "Listen up, people. This, as most of you already know, is Phineas Crane. He's been temporarily released to consult in a joint investigation with the FBI. Anybody who so much as breathes a whisper about this to the public will be fired on the spot *without* severance. Am I clear?"

The officers mumbled an affirmative.

"Excellent. I'm sure either Captain Donovan or myself can answer any questions you may have. As you were."

The captain took Miller aside and looked him square in the eyes. "No unnecessary risks, okay? Come back to us alive and kicking."

"I'll do my best."

Donovan turned to Crane. "It was a mistake to let you live. If anything happens to Miller, I will personally rectify that mistake."

"You'll have to join the queue, I'm afraid," Crane said. "Regardless, you have my word—no harm shall come to him by my hand."

"Or your foot, elbow, teeth, blade or gun?"

Crane smiled. "If we must be pedantic."

"You bet your ass we must."

Half an hour later, Miller sat in the back of the containment van opposite their prisoner, luggage by his foot, blaster in hand resting on his knee. Crane made no attempt to converse and simply sat up straight with his eyes closed.

After a brief detour to allow Collins some packing of his own, Agent Nichols directed him to a restricted airstrip at Thurgood Marshall International. There, the group boarded a federal tiltrotor, modified for business-class level travel, and settled in for the flight.

PART II

CRANE

CHAPTER 9

Twenty-five minutes later, the tiltrotor touched down at Reagan National Airport.

The flight had been uneventful; Miller had split his time between staring out the window and watching Agent Nichols.

From within his jacket, Nichols had produced his personal computer—a small gadget which reminded him of the old ballpoint pens. Setting it down, the agent twisted one end and it lit up, projecting a hard-light laser keyboard onto the table. Sensors detected changes in air pressure, interpreted the motions as keystrokes, sending data to the holographic monitor, which turned opaque, preventing Miller from seeing what he was up to.

At the other end of the cabin, Crane and Collins engaged in a series of chess matches. With each loss, Collins grew more agitated, but thankfully, they came in to land before things could escalate.

An armored M2 Triumph SUV waited for them, which Nichols insisted only he could drive, to the chagrin of Collins.

Once again, Miller sat opposite Crane in the rear-facing seats, replaying the footage.

Despite the poor quality of the video, he managed to get a good look at the impersonator. The exosuit was nearly identical to the one he remembered, albeit slimmer, and while Crane's had been colored a mixture of dark grey and navy blue for blending into the night, this one was jet-black, adorned with flame decals.

"Hardly inconspicuous, are they?" said Crane.

Miller ignored him, focusing on the unfolding scene. Emerging from a similar SUV, the federal agent was talking on his headset, paying little attention to his surroundings. He was at home and off the clock, after all; why shouldn't he let his guard down for a bit?

The victim whirled as the imitator dropped into view. Drawing his sidearm, the agent fired, but his assailant raised his left arm, dispersive plating blocking the bolts, then stepped forward, swinging his right arm. The fingers of the suit's right hand tapered into sharp edges, which sliced cleanly through the gun barrel. Staying in motion, the attacker pivoted, delivering a spinning heel kick, knocking away the remnants of the weapon.

Rather than go in for the kill, he did a little shuffling dance, taunting the man, who lashed out, hitting nothing but air. Again and again, he missed. The attacker was toying with him.

The man lashed out, grabbing the agent's arm and twisting. The agent screamed.

A mechanized elbow slammed into the limb a second time. The attacker jumped backward, spinning, landed on one leg and sprang forward again to kick him in the chest with his other foot.

The agent's head bounced off the door of his car, he fell out of frame and the footage ended.

"He telegraphs his attacks," said Miller. "Why go to all the effort? Why not just shoot him?

"Showmanship?" mused Crane.

"What do you mean?"

"Gladiators in ancient Rome didn't only fight, they had to make a show of it, to entertain a crowd. What if our assailant has an audience?"

"So he records his attacks?"

"Possibly. He could live stream it. Who knows what voyeurs and sadists out there want to see someone murder a federal agent?"

"That explains the suit," said Miller. "He wants attention."

"Precisely, Sergeant. You have your thinking cap on."

"Those sickos probably *pay* to watch, even take bets on how many feds get killed?" Miller looked at Crane. "Was that why you did it? For money?"

Crane glared back. "Of course not. *I* have standards."

"A principled killer is still a killer."

"I am aware, Sergeant, but I'm not trying to justify my actions. Suffice it to say, I had my reasons."

"Whatever you say."

Miller replayed the footage again.

"Collins is wrong about you," Crane said abruptly.

"What?"

"I acknowledge you were—for want of a better term—the clear victor in our first encounter, but it wasn't luck. I severely underestimated you."

"Guess you won't do that again."

"I learned my lesson. You, on the other hand, waited until an opportunity presented itself and seized it. Not many people can turn the tables to their advantage as you did. An admirable trait."

"Crane, if you say anything about how similar we are, I'll break your other arm."

"Perish the thought, Sergeant," Crane said with a smile. "There are some clichés even *I* won't indulge in."

***

Agent Nichols pulled the Triumph up to the J. Edgar Hoover building, winding down the window as a guard approached with a handheld facial recognition scanner. The guard verified

Nichols, Miller and Collins. The agent told the guard that Crane was a criminal being admitted under his supervision. The guard stared at Crane for a moment, then shrugged and waved them through.

"Don't talk to anyone," Nichols ordered. "You especially, Crane."

Few agents were around, proving Nichols hadn't lied when he'd said they'd been stretched thin. Ever since the bureau had been rocked by a series of scandals, they'd struggled to keep hold of their personnel.

He led them to an elevator. They all piled in and he pressed the sub-level button. Miller hoped all this downward travel wasn't indicative of how this mission would pan out.

When the elevator doors opened, it was like walking into a different facility. Sleek and starkly bright, the area looked to be a fairly recent addition to the old building.

"Welcome to the morgue," said Agent Nichols, opening the door.

It was colder than the maximum-security facility, and Miller shivered in his mack. Even Crane looked chilly. They were met by a cheerful, bespectacled woman with exceedingly pale skin. Her mauve hair was pulled back into a ponytail and beneath her lab coat, she wore a t-shirt emblazoned with the name of a band Miller didn't recognize.

"Hey, Greg. What brings you down here?"

"That's *Agent Nichols*, Ms. Shields."

"That's *Doctor* Shields," she shot back. "If we're getting technical."

Nichols closed his eyes and pinched the bridge of his nose, exasperated. "Fine." He sighed and handed over a data drive. "I need you to retrieve the bodies numbered on this drive."

"Whatever happened to 'please?'"

"'Please' is for people with time to waste." Nichols headed back to the door.

"Where are you going?"

"To get warm," he snapped. "I'm freezing my nuts off in here."

Collins, Crane and Miller watched the exchange uncomfortably until he left.

"Sorry about Agent Sunshine. There's a lot on his mind," said the woman. "Like who ate the last bagel in the cafeteria yesterday."

Miller introduced himself and Collins. "Can you help us, please, Doctor?"

"Call me Helena. And since you asked so nicely, yes, I can." She eyed Crane warily. "As long as you tell me what a convicted felon is doing in my lab first."

"Mr. Crane is assisting with the investigation."

"But he's the Metro Mutilator! What if he mutilates me?"

"He's under control," said Collins, putting a hand on the prisoner's shoulder. "He's promised to be on his best behavior, haven't you, Crane?"

"I can assure you, I have no quarrel with medical examiners, Doctor," Crane said.

Helena nodded but kept her distance. Moving to a control panel, she inserted the data drive and hit a few buttons. "Sorry about the temperature, by the way. My enhancement is an abnormally high body temperature."

"You don't feel this at all?" asked Collins.

"Actually, I'm a little warm."

A pneumatic hiss demanded the doctor's attention, and she turned back to the console. A hatch opened in the nearby wall, through which two oblong casket-like containers came.

"Our less-than-state-of-the-art cold chamber," she explained as she fit the caskets to a pair of mobile frames. "You have to manually reset the temperature periodically from inside. I've been lobbying for an upgrade for the better part of the year, but nobody listens."

Helena wheeled one over to the center of the room. Miller brought the other, trying hard not to think too much about who lay inside or what condition they might be in.

The doctor locked the frames into place and switched on the overhead work lights. Breaking the hermetic sealing, she folded down the sides of the caskets, forming tables on which the bodies lay. "Meet Agents Erica Ryan and Herman Schwartz. The last two victims of six so far."

Both bodies were a gruesome sight, and Collins winced. Beneath jagged gashes, bruising and abrasions, Miller recognized the male agent from the surveillance footage.

Crane stared at the wounds.

"There are similarities to your handiwork, Mr. Crane," Helena said. "But, obviously you've been in custody lately."

Picking up a digital pad, she dimmed the lights and activated a holographic projector. Flickering to life, it displayed a logo of a chain and the word "Interm0d," then changed to a query box.

"This is the Intermod Digital Database, currently used by two hundred morgues, nationwide," the doctor explained. "Every photograph taken of a body from the past several years is collated into a giant virtual archive, accessible to anybody who uses this system."

Crane caught on first. "Or if we wanted to see a Baltimore serial killer's victim."

"Exactly. All I need is a case number or a date."

Crane rattled off both automatically. Miller supposed he retained the informational snippet from his trial.

Helena entered the numbers and the image of a body flashed up. A knot formed in Miller's stomach as he recognized the face—Vic Baxter, his former partner. He fought the urge to walk over and perform some impromptu dental-work on Crane. If he wanted a reaction, Miller wouldn't give him one.

"This the guy?" asked Helena.

Miller nodded.

The projection morphed into a full, three-dimensional, near-transparent replica of the body, floating horizontally between the two tables. "Pretty cool, huh?"

Miller wasn't sure that was the word he'd use. Aside from an occasional ripple as pixels settled, the likeness was uncanny. Unsettled, he averted his eyes, while Crane stepped forward.

"Are you sure this was one of yours?" asked Helena. "Where are the wounds?"

"Look at the back," Crane suggested.

Miller glanced again as she rotated the image of Vic until he was facing downward, revealing four puncture marks grouped together in a vertical line, starting from the base of his neck.

"What the hell could have done that?" asked the doctor.

"The same weapon used on your agents," said Crane. "Just utilized differently."

"You're right," she said, after looking closer. "Compare the wounds. Agent Schwartz has been slashed and hacked like a wild animal attacked him, but the cop was killed with a single thrust through the spine and presumably an armored vest. The Mutilator knew what he was doing, but this imposter lacks his restraint. My guess is it's somebody impulsive or who has unresolved anger issues."

"They might be looking for attention," said Crane. "Some perverse online entertainment."

"Ugh." Helena grimaced. "I guess that makes sense. Also, look at these gashes on Schwartz. The angle indicates right-hand dominance, while the position of the wounds on the cop suggests the Mutilator was left-hand dominant."

"I'm ambidextrous, actually," Crane corrected her. "But yes, I used my left."

"So your suspect is right-handed," Helena said. "That narrows it down to most of seven-hundred *thousand* people in D.C. alone."

"We have to start somewhere," said Miller.

"What's with the burns?" Collins asked, abruptly. He pointed to a patch of scorched flesh on Ryan's shoulder.

"I don't know. All the agents' bodies have them somewhere, except for the first, and Agent Schwartz here. If you're going for an up-close and personal kill, why use a ranged weapon?"

"I have an idea," said Crane. "Collins, imagine you're one of these agents, accosted by the person who killed your friends and is now going to kill you. What would you do?"

"Shoot him down," Collins said simply.

"With the blaster in the holster beneath your jacket?"

"Yeah."

"Can you demonstrate?"

"I don't have my blaster."

"Pretend."

"Seriously?"

"I'd do it myself, but my hands aren't exactly free."

Looking highly self-conscious, Collins mimed reaching across his body to draw a blaster with his right hand, aiming the imaginary weapon directly at Crane.

"Sergeant Miller, if you saw someone reaching for their sidearm, how would you react?"

"Drop 'em with a stun shot."

"Assume they're wearing an EDA vest."

"Headshot, then."

"No, don't think like a cop, think like the killer," said Crane. "You want to stop him from grabbing his gun but you don't want to kill him too quickly."

"Disable his arm, I guess."

"That would give the attacker time to close the distance," said Collins.

"Correct," said Crane. "But speaking from personal experience, claws in the suit greatly reduce dexterity. Holding a blaster would be difficult, if not downright impossible, let alone shooting somebody non-fatally."

"You're right," said Helena. "The injuries are more consistent with a cutting laser rather than a blaster or pulse rifle. Those are pretty bulky, though. They'd have to fire a burst, then drop the cutter and risk damaging it. Could it be built into the armor?"

"Shoulder-mounted, I should think," Crane said. "With a wrist-mounted interface."

"There wasn't one in the surveillance footage," said Miller.

"They could have been trying something different for their viewers," said Crane. "Sergeant Miller, how would you describe the attacker's fighting style from the footage?"

"Showy, with a lot of unnecessary jumping."

"A shoulder-mounted cutter would require an external battery to avoid draining the suit's power," said Crane, "which would cut down on their acrobatics. So instead, they use extra dispersive plating to block blaster-fire until they can get close enough."

"Okay, so you're looking for a right-handed man or woman with exceptional athletic ability and a background in martial arts," said Helena, "like a gymnast or a traceur."

"I assume considerably fewer people fit that bill," Crane said.

"So what do we do now?" asked Collins. "Knock on every door around D.C. and ask who spends their free time making kung-fu snuff films?"

"Not quite, Collins," said Crane. "I have a few leads of my own. Come, let's go find our handler."

Collins placed a hand on Crane's shoulder and guided him out of the morgue, taking care to bump him into the doorway as they went. The Englishman did not react.

Before he left, Miller gave the medical examiner his personal number, in case she came up with anything else they might find useful.

"Thank you for your help, Doctor," he said as he headed for the door.

Helena smiled wanly. "And thank you for showing basic courtesy, Sergeant."

CHAPTER 10

Miller stared out the car window at the passing city. The sergeant was out of his element, here. A beat cop through and through, he was used to mobile patrol, guarding a crime scene, responding to a domestic disturbance or even participating in the occasional tactical strike. Detective work felt beyond him. But he had an assignment and prided himself on seeing things through.

"Here we are," said Crane.

Agent Nichols pulled up to the curb opposite a dilapidated public housing complex.

"If you're yanking our chains…" Collins warned.

"A little faith, I beg of you. Singleton is a creature of habit. He's as likely to move as I am to become the next American president. Here he comes now."

A scrawny, sour-faced man scurried down the street toward them, beady eyes darting left and right.

Cutting the engine, Nichols jumped out. "Mr. Singleton?"

The man slowed but said nothing.

"Gregory Nichols, FBI." The agent flashed his ID.

"Don't know anyone by that name," the man said. "Sorry."

"Now, now, Stephen," said Crane, emerging from the vehicle. "Do you want your trousers to catch alight?"

Singleton's eyes grew even wider. "M-mister Crane! You… I… you…" He emitted a fearful wheeze and spun around, only to find his way barred by Collins.

"A word, if we may?" asked Crane, then gestured to his shackled arms. "In private, preferably. You're quite safe, provided you're helpful."

Singleton tried to speak but couldn't seem to get his mouth to work. Nodding instead, he fished out his access card and led them into the old building.

The corridor was empty. "Is this alright?" he asked. "Or do you wanna come up to the top floor?"

"This should do," said Crane.

"Good. Now, what do you want?"

"I need to speak to Layton. Is he still in D.C. or has he moved yet again?"

"I dunno."

"Don't test me, Stephen. You know who I am and what I can do."

"Take it easy, Crane," said Collins. "Don't make me do something you'll regret."

"I'm telling you, I don't know," said Singleton. "Could be he is, could be he ain't. You know how paranoid he gets."

"You're his personal assistant, why wouldn't you know?" asked Crane.

"I *was*, until two months ago, when Norwich up and fires me. No explanation, no severance. Now I'm back to scraping a living hawking frickin' gewgaws to tourists."

"Alright. The last time you saw him, was he still over in Mount Vernon Triangle?"

"Yeah, but like I said, I haven't got a clue if he's still there."

"We might as well check, if only to rule it out. Now, give the nice federal agent a contact number and you can be on your way."

Nichols took out his phone and they initiated a number transfer.

"Got it," the agent said. "Don't leave town."

"Whatever."

Back in the Triumph, Collins turned to Crane. "How do we know he's leveling with us? He could be sending us on a wild goose chase."

"Unlikely. For all his faults, Singleton isn't a convincing liar."

"And how do we know he isn't in league with *you?*"

"And just how might I have contacted him from within maximum security? I didn't even get my one call after I was arrested."

Collins glared but had no reply.

"I suppose you're right not to trust me," said Crane. "But you don't have a lot to go on otherwise. We should keep track of Singleton. He's quite the jack of all trades and could come in handy."

"Who's Layton Norwich?" asked Miller.

"A retired shipping magnate and multi-millionaire. A few years after moving to the States, I tracked him down and ingratiated myself, then used his money to finance the design and manufacture of my suit."

"So how did you get him to agree?"

"I can be quite charming and persuasive when I've a mind to be."

"You had something on him, didn't you?" asked Collins.

"Perhaps."

"Like what?"

"That's between Mr. Norwich and myself, Collins," tutted Crane. "And I'll thank you to stay out of it."

———•———

An impressive feat of architectural engineering, Regal Grande Tower was the opposite of where they'd found Singleton. Every surface of the ornate foyer was pristine and polished to a mirror sheen. Miller preferred the public housing complex.

Nichols approached reception, leaving the others standing by the door. He returned and told them Norwich was still on the books, and he'd acquired an access code for the room.

As they passed by the desk, Miller caught the withering gaze of the concierge in his peripherals and felt self-conscious. Waiting for the elevator, he noticed his crooked tie in the reflection of a gold-plated pillar. He straightened the offending neckwear and could practically hear Marion's voice chiding him in his head. He didn't know if he should take off his coat and hat, or if, in doing so, he risked the staff burning them on principle. He hoped the others wouldn't notice his unease. The elevator was even manned by a smartly uniformed operator.

"Top floor," ordered Nichols, dispensing with basic courtesy once again.

They piled in and the operator set the car in motion. If he noticed the metal shackles worn by Crane, he said nothing, staring solemnly ahead as the lights on the control panel illuminated one by one. If he expected a tip, however, he was to be disappointed, though Miller uttered a quick thanks as they stepped out.

Coming to the suite, Agent Nichols unlocked the door and they followed him in.

Inside, they were met by a man in his early sixties clutching a glass. He wore a satin dressing gown and a tan bordering on orange.

He stared, confusion etched across his face, which grew into fear.

"Hello, Layton," said the Mutilator.

"C-Crane? What are you doing here? Who… who are these people?"

"I'm out on good behavior," Crane replied, "and these are my chaperones."

Norwich nodded dumbly.

"Well?" Crane continued. "Where's your sense of hospitality, Layton? Aren't you going to offer them a drink, or have you polished it all off yourself?"

"I… I don't…"

"Do stop babbling, man!"

Holding his head, Norwich sat on the nearby sofa and took a few moments to gather himself. "What do you want, Crane?"

"The Wraith power suit you had made for me. I need three more for my associates here. Same specifications, but customized measurements, of course."

"I can't."

"Why ever not?"

"I… er… sold the blueprints."

"What? To whom?"

"I can't tell you. Buyer confidentiality."

"That was *not* our agreement, Layton," Crane said, an edge in his voice.

"You were in jail!" said Norwich. "Look, why don't we all have a drink and work something out? I could build you an even better suit for you and your buddies."

"Very well." Crane sighed. "Do you have any of that '64 Appalachian Sherry left?"

Norwich smiled. "Half a bottle."

"Three glasses then. And tonic water for Mr. Miller."

Miller grimaced. He would have almost preferred alcohol.

Wobbling ever so slightly, Norwich made his way over to the drinks table. "I *would* give Singleton the day off," he muttered as he poured.

Miller looked at Crane, who was watching their host closely.

As they drank, Norwich lit an expensive-looking cigar. A real one, no electronics or vapor here. Miller thought about how Vic Baxter would have loved one of those.

Agent Nichols sipped his sherry, while Collins quaffed his in one go, obviously accustomed to harder drinks. Miller eyed his glass in distaste.

Crane savored his sherry down to the last drop. "'Now that,' as Cousin Don would say, 'is a bloody good drop.' And with that out of the way, onto the next point of order. Gentlemen, if you would be so kind as to draw your weapons. We are dealing with an imposter."

Something in his matter-of-fact tone affirmed truth, and both men had their sidearms in hand and aimed at Norwich in a flash.

Startled, Norwich almost dropped his cigar. "What the hell?"

"You'd better be damned sure about this, Crane," said Nichols.

"Quite sure. We are looking at a fraud. A fraud with an exact likeness to Layton, but a fraud nonetheless."

"That's ridiculous," said Norwich.

"Hardly. You've done well, no doubt fooling many people, myself almost included. But you overlooked a few minor— yet crucial—details.

"The *real* Layton and I were on first name terms. Then there's your voice. Your cadence, timbre and inflections are impressively accurate, but you've yet to fully develop the telling rasp of a lifelong smoker. Norwich is right-handed, whereas you poured with, drank with, and lit your cigar with your left.

"Finally, you mentioned giving Singleton the day off, but we talked to him earlier. He claims you fired him months ago."

Norwich just stared.

"Considering Singleton had worked with Norwich for so long, he would have cottoned on to your little deception," continued Crane. "You needed him out of the picture without killing him and risking attention. So you fired him."

Personally, having never met Norwich, Miller couldn't verify Crane's claims. But he'd seen the look etched onto the man's face many times over his career. The look of somebody who knew the game was up.

CHAPTER 11

Crane looked at the imposter. "It's simple. The more cooperative you are, the more charitable *we* are."

Not-Norwich sat on a high-back barstool, bound with the cord from his own dressing gown, looking petrified.

"If you refuse," continued Crane, "things will become unpleasant for you."

"You… you can't do this. I have rights!"

"Which you waived by committing identity theft." Crane turned to the others. "Gentlemen, you should search the premises."

"You can't!" the imposter yelled, panicked.

"Why ever not?" asked Crane. "Sergeant Miller is an officer of the law and is legally entitled to do so."

"Not without a search warrant."

"Probable cause," Miller said.

The man in the chair closed his eyes tightly. "You're right, I'm not Norwich," he said, wearily. "My name is Sweetman."

"Your guise is impeccable," said Crane. "I'm curious. Did you cosmetically alter yourself or do you just happen to resemble him?"

Sweetman said nothing.

"It could be Semblatex makeup," said agent Nichols. "They can do incredible things with prosthetics in Hollywood these days."

"Or, for a simpler explanation," said Crane, "we are dealing with an enhanced, correct?"

Sweetman averted his eyes.

"I'll take that as a yes. Fascinating. I've heard of shapeshifters, but never actually met one. And you can alter your vocal cords to match theirs. I wonder, does that extend to DNA, or does it remain your own?"

"Admire the freak later, Crane," said Collins. "Let's get some answers."

"Of course," Crane said. "Well, Mr. Sweetman, have you anything to say for yourself?"

"I impersonate certain kinds of people. Mostly people who need to be seen somewhere else."

"An alibi?"

"Exactly. Anyway, this guy hired me to replace Norwich at fifty-thousand standard per week, indefinitely. I normally don't take jobs that long, but the money was too good."

"Who hired you?"

"Never met 'em. There was a middle-man, but I never got his name. They just told me to talk as little as possible to people, and the money came in from a private account."

"Thank you for being so forthcoming," said Crane. "Though that does beg the question, where *is* Layton?"

"I've found him," said Miller.

He led them to a chest freezer in the laundry room.

Inside lay the frozen, contorted body of the real Layton Norwich. Judging by the bruising around his neck, he'd been strangled.

Nichols blanched at the sight, while Collins whistled, impressed. "Damn. Didn't think our friend out there had it in him to murder a guy."

They went back into the lounge room.

"There's a man who looks an awful lot like you in the freezer," Crane said. "Care to explain?

"I didn't kill him," Sweetman said. "He was dead when I arrived."

"Either way, I think it's time we saw your real face, don't you?"

"Whether you killed him or not, wearing his face is tantamount to pissing on his body."

"He has a point, Mr. Sweetman," said Miller. "You ought to change back."

"It's been months. My body's reconfigured itself to this form."

"Try."

"No."

"For crying out loud!" said Collins, drawing his sidearm. "Shift it!"

"I don't want to. It'll be agony!"

Thumbing the ID pad, Collins placed the muzzle of his blaster against his knee. "Worse than this?"

Placing his other hand over Sweetman's mouth, he fired. Sweetman screamed.

"That was over the line, Collins," said Miller.

"He should have cooperated."

Crane saw the sergeant glare at Collins but knew he wouldn't rock the boat. Meanwhile, Sweetman's scream had faded to a muffled sob. Collins released him.

"Shut up, Sweetman. You still have another kneecap." Collins pressed the gun to the other knee. "As long as you do what we say."

Sweetman nodded, screwing his eyes shut.

They heard a nauseating cracking sound and he gasped in pain, skin rippling as bones shifted and re-knit themselves. His spine elongated with a series of pops, his nose, ears and lower jaw narrowed with a grinding crunch, and his hair fell out in clumps.

The tan faded as his complexion lightened, his hair re-growing a light auburn, thick and curly. Crane hadn't expected it to be so gruesome.

A final shudder and a new person sat before them, who threw up, then passed out.

Agent Nichols looked a little green around the gills himself.

"Pathetic," Collins said, holstering his weapon. "Now what?"

"We'd better call this in." Miller reached for his phone.

Nichols stopped him. "No, Sergeant. The last thing we need is this place being turned into a crime scene."

"Homicide is a crime, last time I checked," said Miller. "Which means this *is* a crime scene."

"Don't get fresh with me, Sergeant. You're forgetting the pecking order here."

Miller glared at him. Funny how he only showed some spine when it came to people supposedly on his side.

"Our case takes priority," he continued. "Alerting the authorities will result in an investigation. They can try to be discreet, but sooner or later a nosy neighbor will see what's going on, or some wet-eared rookie will accidentally spill the beans. Next thing you know, the local news gets wind of it and we'll have a nine-ring media circus here for the dead multi-millionaire recluse. When that happens, you can bet whoever's responsible is gonna see it and skip town."

"Good Lord!" said Crane. "He actually makes a valid point; we must assume the killer and the buyer of the blue-prints are linked."

It was a reasonable assumption. If the copycat killer had commissioned an identical suit and taken the blueprints, it wasn't inconceivable they would kill Norwich to ensure his silence.

Crane took the opportunity to wander the apartment in case anything jumped out at him. As he looked, he listened to the others.

"So what are we going to do about the shapeshifter?" Miller asked. "Do we ask him politely to stay put while we continue our investigation?"

"We'll take him to the Met Police on a drunk and disorderly charge," said Nichols. "That gets him out of the way without drawing attention to the body."

"What's to stop him from blabbing?" asked Collins.

"We outline his options. Either he buttons up and stays in a nice safe cell, we turf him out to take his chances with his employer, or he finds himself blacklisted from the whole country."

Miller sighed. "So now we've incapacitated our best lead, what next?"

Nichols stopped to think. "Search the place anyway. We might find something."

Crane stopped in the kitchen, and looked at the refrigerator, specifically the holographic screen on the door. There was a message left on the vidphone, converted to text.

"Gentlemen, I believe I may have found something."

"What is it?" asked Miller.

Crane beckoned them over to the kitchen and pointed at the message.

```
Be at Danton's tomorrow night. Boss
wants to chat. No cops. Be smart.
```

The notification had arrived an hour earlier, and it seemed Sweetman had elected to ignore it. Attached was a digital invitation addressed to Layton Norwich. Evidently, he'd been invited to some kind of soiree by one Charles Danton—DuroCorp senior shareholder and D.C. socialite.

"Do they think they're dealing with the real Norwich or do they want Sweetman?" Miller wondered aloud.

"Either way, the mystery client will be at the party," Crane said. "If we can ingratiate ourselves into the proceedings, we may be a step closer to uncovering our copycat killer.

He knelt beside the shapeshifter and examined the knee. "Fascinating. It's completely healed! The transformation process must occur on a cellular level."

"How does a dead man go to a party?" asked Collins.

Crane smiled knowingly. "Leave that to me."

Soon after midnight, Miller took a stroll around the nearby Adams Morgan strip. They'd dropped Sweetman at the nearest police station, and since neither Collins nor he belonged to the precinct and were off-duty, they dealt with no paperwork, to the dismay of one unlucky DCMP officer.

Afterward, the four men checked in to their hotel. Agent Nichols had two rooms booked, putting himself in one and Crane, Collins, and Miller in the other. Their room contained only one bedroom with a single bed, so Miller worked out a system. One of them would take the bed, while the other would stay in the living room to watch Crane, whom they locked outside on the balcony.

Collins had a pair of handcuffs, an old-fashioned pair of steel braclets with a connecting chain, requiring a key to unlock rather than the thumbprint of the arresting officer. He attached one shackle to Crane's ankle, and the other to the heavy metal chair. Crane wouldn't be going anywhere, and if he tried undoing the cuff, he'd get a stun bolt in the chest for his trouble.

Collins took the first watch, so Miller retired to the bedroom. As a precaution, he wedged a chair up under the old-fashioned door-handle before settling down for a fitful snooze.

Six hours later, the alarm on his phone sounded and he was up again. Out of politeness to Collins, he'd elected to sleep on the floor and now paid for it. Trying to massage some feeling back into his stiff joints, he walked back out to the living room.

Collins paced back and forth, muttering to himself and tapping his fingers against the butt of his sidearm at his hip. Outside, Crane sat with his back up against the balcony.

"I'm getting some coffee," he told Collins. "I'll be back before one."

"You'd better be," Collins replied under his breath.

Miller passed a handful of bars and nightclubs as he walked. Some patrons patiently queued outside, waiting to be let in, others staggered out, looking for a cab or heading next door. All of them were much younger than him.

A billboard projected a fifty-foot tall holographic image promoting the latest Chad Savage blockbuster. Miller recalled the time electronic screen boards had been the norm. He'd even seen a few older ones where the advertisement needed to be stuck to the board with an adhesive substance. How times had changed.

With a shimmer, the image changed, stopping Miller in his tracks. The ad in question was a black-and-white promotion for a production at the Lincoln Theatre.

Endgame by Samuel Beckett.

The timing was like a sick cosmic joke. Memories of Marion rushed back and slapped him in the face. His legs turned to lead and he felt a familiar, unwelcome stinging behind his eyes. *Why here? Why now? Why* this *play?*

Standing in the middle of the sidewalk, he had never felt so alone.

The hologram shimmered again and changed to an animated antacid commercial, breaking his trance.

I can't go on. I'll go on.

Pushing by, Miller moved down the street, coming to a Hopper's diner, where he purchased three extra-large cups of straight black coffee and a couple of pastries.

Arriving back at the hotel at ten to one, he relieved Collins early.

"I'm going to the bar," Collins told him. "Don't worry, I'll call Conway in a few hours."

Out on the balcony, Crane hadn't moved, though his eyes were now open and watchful.

Even though it invited the possibility of dozing off, Miller sat down on the couch. Grabbing the first cup, he took a sip and stared right back.

CHAPTER 12

Collins returned around three o'clock, more or less sober, to Miller's surprise. He declined an offer for the third cup of now-tepid coffee, retiring to the bedroom instead.

The rest of the shift passed without incident. The only time Crane made a sound was a polite request to be allowed a bathroom break. Miller cleared everything out of the bathroom that wasn't bolted down, leaving nothing more than a pile of toilet paper sheets, and gave him two minutes. Crane was done in one. Miller supervised the hand-washing at gunpoint, then escorted him back outside.

At eight, Collins returned to the living room and took over for Miller, who hit the shower, then the streets. Still buzzed from the caffeine, he knew he'd regret choosing not to sleep later, but he'd worry about that when it happened.

Stopping in at Greasy McGee's, he ordered two servings of hotcakes and two cups of orange juice to go. Arriving at the police station where they'd left Sweetman, he requested to see the enhanced.

Time to play the "good cop."

Since even plastic utensils were not allowed, they rolled up their hotcakes, dipping them in the syrup and whipped cream. Sweetman attacked his with voracity, and Miller ended up ceding his last one to the starved man.

He watched as Sweetman guzzled both cups of juice and used a finger to scoop the last remnants from his little container of cream.

"Sorry about Collins," said Miller. "I'm sure you noticed he has some anger issues."

"Understatement," muttered Sweetman.

"You got off lightly." Miller thought back to the extensive bruising he'd seen on Crane. "You said you didn't kill Norwich?"

"That's right."

"Then who did?"

"Some guy."

"That doesn't help."

"It's all I know." Sweetman shrugged. "It was done when I arrived. The guy made me help him shove the body into the fridge. When we were done, he told me he'd come around again to make sure I did what I was told and that I hadn't blabbed. He left, and I went and puked in the sink."

Miller didn't blame him. Sweetman was prepared for identity theft, not hiding a body. No wonder he'd hit the booze so hard.

"What did the guy look like?"

"Six foot three, maybe four, all muscle. Short blond hair, icy grey eyes."

"Any other distinguishing features?"

"Yeah, he had a surgical scar running down the middle of his nose. He looked ex-military," said Sweetman. "He didn't talk much except to bark orders."

"Could he have been the guy who contracted you?"

"Nah. Hired muscle, if anything."

"How many times did he come back to check on you?"

"Three or four times, the last being a week ago. I tried locking the doors, but he had an override code."

Miller rubbed at his chin. "Someone as paranoid as Norwich would have had security cameras inside."

Sweetman confirmed this, but they'd been deactivated by the man. Miller grimaced. It wasn't much to go on.

"What's going to happen to me?" asked Sweetman.

"Not my call. You're here for your own protection. Just sit tight for now and try not to draw attention to yourself."

"Okay. Thanks for breakfast."

Miller nodded. "Sure thing."

———————•———————

Outside, Miller noticed a missed call from Captain Donovan. He rang back as he waited in line at a coffee stall.

"How's it going, Myles?"

"Slowly," he said and filled her in.

"One step forward, two steps back, eh?"

"Sure feels that way. The shindig at this Danton guy's place could get us somewhere."

"Here's hoping," she sighed. *"Look, just nail the bastard, put Crane back in his hole and come home asap, okay? The chief is getting antsy."*

"You don't think he'd actually fire us, do you?"

"If the commissions board don't like our progress, he won't have to. We need every result we can get, Myles."

"I'll do my best."

No sooner had Miller ended the call than his phone rang again. An unknown number; he answered anyway. "Hello?"

"Sergeant Miller?"

"Dr. Shields. Thank you for calling."

"I've found something which I think could really help."

"What have you got?"

"Get this—after I went home, I couldn't stop thinking about the scorch marks. Why do only four of the six bodies have them?"

"I thought they scrapped the mounted laser in favor of mobility?"

"So why did it take them four more victims to realize that? After the second or even third, I could understand. So, what if it had to do with height? Agent Schwartz was short for a man his

age; five-foot-six. Assuming the laser couldn't be adjusted easily, maybe our perp was too tall."

"Doctor, do you think you could get to the point?" asked Miller, patiently.

"Right. I compared the four agents side by side. Each scorch mark was on the same side on slightly different parts of the body. I measured each position, and they're all the same. I'd say your copycat killer is no more than five foot eleven."

"That does narrow it down a bit. There are still a few thousand who'd match that description, but we'll have a better idea of what to keep an eye out for. Thanks again, Doctor. Please, keep me in the loop if you find anything else."

"Will do."

———•———•———

Miller knocked on the door of Nichols' room, cardboard coffee tray in hand; a peace offering.

Nichols answered the door, bleary-eyed and frowning. "What do you want, Sergeant?"

"Good morning, Agent Nichols. Coffee?"

"No. I can't stand the stuff."

Miller felt his eye twitch. "Suit yourself. I may have another lead."

He relayed the new information from both Dr. Shields and Sweetman, helping himself to the second coffee.

"Alright," said Nichols. "Make sure you tell the others. We'll keep an—"

A crash from the other room cut him off. Cursing, Miller pushed the coffee cup into Nichol's hand, drew his sidearm and rushed to the door. Steeling himself, he flung it open, blaster at the ready.

He expected to find Collins lying on the floor, bleeding out from a slashed throat, or worse, and Crane standing over his body with a bloodied pen or rusty couch spring. Maybe he'd even use his teeth.

Instead, it was Crane who was half-sprawled on the carpet. Collins stood over him, gripping the collar of his uniform in one hand, bringing down the other to punch him again with a dull, wet crack. Though bruised and bloody, Crane remained expressionless.

Almost mesmerized, Miller watched as Collins hit him again and again, before catching himself. "Collins!"

The ex-cop turned. Miller saw the tell-tale tinge of yellow in his eyes; his nose bled.

"Back off, Miller!" he snapped. "He deserves it!"

"Stand down, Collins," Miller ordered.

He ignored him and struck Crane again. Striding toward the pair, Miller holstered his sidearm. He grabbed Collins by the shoulder, who lashed out. Miller brought his left arm up, blocking the blow, then hit him with a satisfying right-cross, snapping his head to the side.

Collins grunted and swung out with a haymaker. Miller ducked, hitting him in the side, just below the rib-cage, then again in the abdomen.

Grabbing him by the arm and lapel of his jacket, Miller twisted and flung him back onto the couch. "Stay down."

Collins, disoriented, didn't move.

Breathing heavily, Miller looked down at Crane. "Are you okay?"

"I'll live," he replied. "You might be in a bit of trouble, however."

Miller followed his gaze, simultaneously becoming aware of a sharp stabbing on his right side. There, jutting out of his forearm, was the syringe tip of a Stimz pen.

CHAPTER 13

Miller stared at the needle in disbelief. Collins must have still been holding the auto-injector when he'd intervened. He yanked out the needle tip, but he already felt strange.

"Tell me that was empty."

Collins said nothing, and Miller knew it hadn't been. His head swam and he leaned against the couch.

He tried to remember what he'd learned from the narcotics officers. Stimz were an artificial stimulant comprised primarily of Hydroponzyloxin, which affected the endocrine system, increasing hormone output and distribution throughout the body.

Miller was in for a ride.

He experienced a rush of sensations—simultaneously bemused, furious and concerned. At the same time, he felt more energized than he had in days, even months. He was on edge but felt a surge of confidence.

He rounded on Collins. "Idiot! What's the matter with you?"

"Take it easy, Miller," he said, truculent. "Don't make me do something you'll regret."

Miller ignored him and began pacing. "Of all the moronic, irresponsible, bone-headed, amateur-hour crap you could have pulled." He babbled as thoughts came fast and fragmented. "Did you even stop to consider… I can't believe you would… how can you possibly justify…?"

"Trust me, Miller, you're gonna want to sit. You'll freak out."

"Nonsense, I feel fine. Don't change the subject. You know Stimz are contraband, but here you are cranking up when you know that that's not allowed. We're escorting a dangerous criminal and you're off your face, and now I'll be too!

"And you're asking for trouble beating on him. When he escapes, he's gonna kill you and he's gonna kill me and he's gonna kill Greg and he's gonna kill Fiona and he's gonna kill all of us."

"I told you, you're freaking out."

"I'm not. I'm actually pumped. I'm ready to go out and kick ass and get this case solved so I can go home and feed my fishy."

Where had that come from?

"You're losing it," said Collins. Or was Miller a mind-reader now?

"I'm good," insisted Miller.

But his body said otherwise. His heart hammered away in his chest. Painfully. His breath came in short, shallow bursts. He couldn't feel his legs and he didn't remember sitting on the floor. He fumbled with the top button on his shirt.

"What… what…" But he couldn't finish his sentence.

And how did he get on his back?

"Collins, what's happening?" asked Nichols, frozen to the spot.

"It's all that coffee," said Collins. "You're not supposed to inject Stimz within twenty-four hours of consuming caffeine."

Miller felt something pressing against his chest. It was the head of Phineas Crane.

"You're cold," Miller muttered.

The head lifted off his chest.

"Tachycardia," Crane said. His voice sounded distant.

You're tachycardia, Miller thought.

"Pick him up," he heard Crane say.

Strong arms lifted Miller from the floor. Someone said something he didn't quite make out, and one of the arms snaked around his neck, choking him.

Heeeey! Nobody heard him.

He tried struggling, but his body wasn't cooperating.

The arm tightened and he lapsed into unconsciousness as easily as slipping into a warm bath.

Collins hadn't really understood the explanation Crane had given, but the gist was that they had to get Miller's heartrate down. Under suggestion from the killer, Collins had put Miller into a sleeper-hold, applying pressure to his carotid artery, restricting the flow of blood to his brain, and subsequently the heart.

"We need to get him to a hospital," said Nichols.

"And who's going to take him in?" Crane asked. "The drug addict, the serial killer or the man who authorized his release?"

Collins felt the sergeant going limp.

Crane took hold of Miller's arm, feeling his pulse. "It's slowing. That should do, let him go now."

But Collins refused.

"Collins, that's enough!"

Collins applied more pressure. He had a chance to shut the sanctimonious Miller up for good.

Then he felt the hardened DuroPlas barrel of a blaster press against his temple. Freezing, he glanced down, saw the empty holster, and realized Crane was holding his own side-arm on him.

"Last warning," he said. "Let Sergeant Miller go before I do to you what you wish you could to me."

"You'll pay for this, Crane," Collins said through gritted teeth.

"Miller is the only thing keeping you alive. *Put. Him. Down.*"

Releasing the chokehold, he carefully lowered Miller to the floor and rolled him into the recovery position. Slowly, he straightened up again, tempted to try disarming Crane, but the Englishman had stepped out of reach.

For the first time, he noticed Nichols fumbling for a compact personal defense blaster.

Despite the artificial confidence Stimz gave him, Collins knew he was at a disadvantage. "I need a drink." He backed toward the door, eyes on the others and their weapons. He gave a mock-bow before turning and exiting the room.

———•

Crane exhaled, relieved, and placed the blaster onto the modest dining table. Glad to be rid of the cretin, he saw that Nichols now pointed the weapon at him. The agent's eyes were wide and Crane saw the telltale shake of his hand.

"I don't suppose you'd assist me getting the sergeant up onto the couch?" he asked, but Nichols made no move.

With injuries of his own, bound hands and the dead-weight of a heavier man, he struggled, but finally managed to get Miller lying on the couch. Checking his pulse and breathing once more and satisfied the sergeant was more or less in the clear, he returned to the balcony and took up the Lotus position again. Only after locking the door behind him again did Nichols put away his gun.

———•

When Miller came around, he saw Crane watching him.

"Welcome back, Sergeant," he said. "You've been out for the better part of an hour."

"What happened?"

Crane filled him in. "If I were a betting man, I'd wager you'll be giving up caffeine."

"You'd lose that bet." It was then he realized that Crane was sitting *inside* at the dining room table. He went for his sidearm, but it was gone. He searched frantically for either of his guns until the room started spinning and he had to close his eyes.

"They're over here," said Crane.

Miller froze, breath coming in ragged gasps. *How did this happen?*

As though reading his mind, Crane answered him. "Collins stalked off to find a bar and forgot to cuff me again. Nichols disappeared a few minutes later." He opened a hand to reveal an access card. "I took this from Collins during all that unpleasantness earlier and let myself in."

Miller waited for the room to stop moving. "Why are you still here?"

Crane hesitated, as though unsure himself.

"I suppose I felt obliged to oversee your recovery," he said at last and gestured to the UCP on the table. "Nor could I resist a closer examination of your ballistic firearm. It's a thing of beauty. Heckler & Koch, yes?"

Miller said nothing.

"Another relic of a bygone era." Crane sighed.

"What happens now?"

Crane leaned back in his chair. "That would depend on you, Sergeant. You can make a move for one of your guns and, given your current state, likely trip and 'eat floor,' while I make my getaway. Alternatively, you stay put and we hold a civilized discussion."

Weighing up both options, Miller chose the latter. "I'll stay put as long as you don't try to put a bullet into me."

"Even if I could handle the damn thing, I've no reason to kill you."

Miller smirked. "Let me guess, your principles?"

"I know you find it hard to believe, but I've never killed indiscriminately."

"No. Just cops. My people."

"In the same profession as you, yes, but these were not your peers."

"How do you figure?"

Crane interlaced his fingers with those of his prosthetic. "Despite your gruff exterior and a fatalistic streak, Sergeant, you remain a man of integrity. You serve and protect to the best of your ability, you respect the badge you wear and the power behind it, and you do not allow your temper to get the better of you."

"Not always," replied Miller, thinking back to his treatment of Modsy the day before.

"My point being," continued Crane, "you are, for all intents and purposes, lawful good. As long as you remain that way, I will make no move against you."

Miller was reluctant to take anything a serial killer said at face value, but at the same time, he couldn't shake the nagging sensation the man was right. "Seems to be a sore point for you."

"I wasn't always Phineas Crane," came the reply. "Until a few years ago, he didn't even exist. I was a different man."

"Who were you, then?"

Crane smiled. "I like you, Sergeant, but not that much."

Miller nodded, then yawned. In spite of himself, he could feel his head growing heavier. He was weary from his near-death experience and his throat hurt from where Collins had applied the chokehold.

"You threatened Collins with his own gun," he said. "But the ID pad prevents anyone other than the owner from firing it."

"Stimz cloud one's perception," said Crane. "He wasn't exactly in a state of mind to call my bluff."

Satisfied, Miller allowed his eyes to close—ignoring the part of his brain warning him not to let down his defense—and fell asleep on the couch.

CHAPTER 14

Miller woke up just as Collins and Nichols returned mid-afternoon. *Good*, he thought, *Collins can watch Crane; I'm wiped*, followed by, *Where's Crane?*

He sat up, looking for him, but Crane was sitting outside, manacled and seated in the Lotus position, as though he'd never moved.

"You awake, Miller?" asked Collins.

"Unfortunately."

Evidently, the Stimz incident would go unmentioned. Miller stood with a groan and headed to the kitchen for a glass of water. As he walked, he noticed both guns were back in his holsters.

"I dropped my access card," said Collins. "Have you seen it?"

Miller couldn't answer. Collins looked to the balcony, gears turning in his head. If he suspected Crane had the card, there would be another beating, and Miller didn't have the strength to intervene again. Looking down, he noticed something poking out of his shirt pocket. He reached in and drew out the access card.

"I have it. Found it when I woke up earlier. You should be more careful."

"Whatever," said Collins, taking the card and gazing at him. For a moment, Miller swore he suspected something.

Nichols spoke, breaking the tension. "Bring Crane in. We need to discuss what's happening tonight."

"I'll do it." Miller made his way to the door. Thankfully, Collins hadn't seemed to notice it wasn't locked. He sat Crane down on the couch before settling on the armchair opposite, sidearm trained on him.

"Danton's event is our best bet to gather information," said Nichols. "With that said, who will go?"

Miller almost snorted. Schmoozing with the upper-crust sounded right up Nichols' alley, so why bother asking the others? Unless he was afraid of encountering the killer in person.

"We should all go," Crane said. "The more ears to the ground we have, the more we'll find out."

"What, and let you mix with civilians?" said Collins. "I don't think so."

"Crane has never targeted civilians," Miller countered. "Besides, if we do run into the copycat, we'll stand a better chance together if things get heavy."

He didn't mention that he didn't trust either of them to watch Crane.

The final decision came down to Nichols, who sided with Crane. Presumably, he just wanted the investigation to be over so he could reap the rewards sooner.

"It's settled then. We all go to Danton's," said Nichols. "So, tell us, Crane, how do we get in on someone else's invite?"

Crane smiled. "Leave that to me."

*   *   *

An hour later, Miller opened the door for Stephen Singleton, who had a carry case in hand and a cabin bag behind him.

"Thank you for coming so promptly, Stephen," said Crane. "So have I got this right? You want me to make you look like Norwich so you can get into a party?"

"Yes. It'd be a mite suspicious if we turned up with his invitation but not the man himself."

"Alright. Take a seat."

Singleton, whose varied occupations at one point had included makeup artist for a number of movies, had come to transform one of them into the dead man. Crane had the closest build, so he sat in a chair under watchful eyes as Singleton worked his magic with Semblatex prosthetic putty. As the putty dried, Singleton took three sets of body measurements for the dinner suits they would need, then provide them to a rental outlet he knew could process orders on short notice.

When the Semblatex was ready, Singleton added colored contact lenses, a synthetic hairpiece and a fake tan.

Given their limited time, the end result was a passable resemblance to the deceased, which had an unsettling effect. At a moderate distance, the disguise was fine, but up close, it looked slightly off. They decided that if anybody asked, they'd explain it away as botched plastic surgery, and yes, he planned to sue. Hopefully, it'd be enough to fool any facial scanners.

Using a few voice messages form the real Norwich, Crane repeated the same sentences, mimicking inflections, pitch and accent until his voice was almost a perfect match. As a practice run, he rang the Regal Grande hotel as Norwich to tell the staff he was placing himself under a self-imposed quarantine for a few days and was not to be disturbed.

"Are you planning to keep me in these restraints?" asked Crane, still practicing with his new voice. "They might raise suspicion."

"How do we know you won't cause trouble?" asked Nichols.

"I know better than to cause a scene around people of this caliber. And I want to uncover my imposter as much as any of you."

"I'll keep him in line," said Collins, which reminded Miller of the microcapsules. The thought made him just as uneasy as it had when Collins had first mentioned them. But then again, they might be the only way to stop Crane, if they were indeed real.

●——————————●

It was almost eight in the evening by the time they arrived via limousine, driven by Singleton. Anybody who saw them couldn't have known that, only an hour earlier, they'd been involved in another tense standoff as Miller had released Crane, covered by both Collins and Nichols.

Thankfully, Crane remained on his best behavior. Eventually, Agent Nichols had relented and arranged for the DC Metropolitan Police to send several unmarked cars to the location as backup.

In an effort to look presentable, Miller had showered and shaved before suiting up. Marion had always said he looked fetching in a tuxedo, but they made him feel restricted. Still, he had to admit, he looked sharp.

Nichols wore his like he was born in it, and even Collins scrubbed up nicely, though he refused to take off his aviators. They had allowed Crane four minutes to shower and dress, though he'd had some difficulty getting his prosthetic arm through the sleeves.

The residence had once been the Josephine Butler Parks Centre until Charles Danton bought them out for a princely eighty million standard. Miller and Collins joined the others in line behind a woman whose dress probably cost more than their annual salaries combined and tried their best to look as though they belonged.

As they passed into the foyer, they saw security was tighter. Unlike the bored-looking guards that manned the perimeter fence, the two inside were hyper-alert and physically formidable. Neither were shorter than six foot, they sported uniform butch cuts, and they carried themselves as men who were more than capable in a fight. They wore black-market DigiComms. Miller noted their identical, icy-grey eyes. Just like the man who'd accosted Sweetman.

Attached to the lapels of their jackets were nametags reading "Dave" and "Joe," accompanied by a scarlet wolfs head insignia.

Collins swore just loud enough for the others in his group to hear but did not elaborate.

"Invite?" asked Dave.

Crane held up the phone, displaying the six-digit verification number. Dave entered the number into his digital pad, bringing up the name and face of Layton Norwich.

"Hold still," said Joe, pointing the handheld facial scanner at Crane. The device beeped, and the guard looked at the screen.

"Eighty-nine percent match."

Crane shrugged nonchalantly. "Don't get work done in Detroit."

"We're gonna have to take a fingerprint scan, sir."

Miller cursed inwardly. The body of the real Norwich had sustained too much damage from the freezer to yield a reliable print for them to copy. They'd hoped they wouldn't be asked.

"Is that necessary?" Crane asked.

"We gotta know you're who you say you are," said Dave.

"This is ridiculous!" Crane made a show of tapping his foot against the polished marble floor. "I demand to see Charles Danton. You can explain to him why you turned away one of his oldest friends."

The guard looked at the line of people behind them, growing ever-restless. The look on his face told Miller they weren't getting paid enough to deal with this. Joe, meanwhile, had stepped away to make a call on his DigiComm.

"Just let 'em through," he said. "Boss says it's okay."

"Whatever," replied Dave, motioning them through and into the main hall.

CHAPTER 15

Inside, the party was well underway. Close to a hundred guests milled about in their evening best, chattering and laughing with varying degrees of sincerity. Waitstaff bustled about with trays of food and drink, while a live band and DJ played rousing electro-swing, which was currently enjoying a resurgence in popularity.

A handful of nondescript guards were dotted around the room, not quite managing to remain inconspicuous. Two more specialists with grey eyes didn't even bother disguising their presence.

"Those guys are bad news," Collins muttered. Big as they were, Collins was bigger still. But if they had him concerned…

"Who are they?" Crane said, equally quiet.

"Mars Group," said Collins. "Mercenaries."

"Are they enhanced?" asked Miller.

"No, but they're so cranked up, they might as well be."

Miller decided he didn't want to know how Collins was privy to that information, instead asking if they were on Stimz.

"Even better. Burnout."

While Stimz use was either restricted or merely frowned upon in most states, Burnout—metamonocluptose—was outright banned nationwide. Taken in tab form, Burnout blocked adenosine receptors in the brain, preventing drowsiness and allowing the user to stay awake for lengthy periods of time. It enhanced sensory awareness and dulled pain-receptors, artificially increasing the body's stamina.

Originally developed for front-line soldiers, a study had found it considerably shortened the lifespan of the user. Presumably, the mercenaries weren't concerned.

It explained the identical colored lenses; not only intimidating, they hid the discolored irises associated with the drug.

"Why do I get the feeling we'll be getting closely acquainted with them before the night is through?" whispered Crane.

Miller agreed. "Try not to kill anybody tonight."

Collins tailed Crane like a bodyguard, and Nichols went off on his own. Fighting the urge to tear open his top button, Miller made his way to the bar and ordered a glass of water with plenty of ice. His mouth felt dry. The plasma burn scar flared up again, but this time, his whole body itched. Was it a side-effect of his encounter with Stimz or was it all in his head?

Somebody called to him and he whipped around. His water had arrived. He reached for his currency token, but the bartender reminded him that it was an open bar. He thanked him and moved on. He felt the bartender's eyes on him, or it might have been the itching.

The ice water helped, but he really wanted coffee. A few more hours without and the headaches would start, which made him think about the Stimz again. He knew it was the addition of sillothocine that gave them their addictive quality. Would he experience withdrawal symptoms? How many hits did it take to get hooked? One? More? He brought up his glass to drink, but it was already empty.

Looking around, he spotted a familiar face. Lin Changi was the CEO of Star Five Enterprises, the company that had designed Crane's exosuit. Their reputation had been severely damaged by the association, forcing them to close their tech division and focus solely on cosmetics.

Around his own age, she wore a modest yet elegant black evening gown, silver-streaked hair pulled back into an elaborate style he didn't recognize. She might even know if anybody else had purchased the blueprints.

Forcing what he hoped was a winning smile onto his face, he approached her. "Ms. Changi?"

She looked up, startled, but quickly pasted on a much more convincing smile. "Yes?"

"Sergeant Miller, BMPD."

The smile wilted. "Oh God, you worked the Metro Mutilator case, didn't you? Look, I'm so sorry about what happened to your people, but I swear we didn't know what the suit was going to be used for."

He doubted there were many benign uses for a mechanized combat suit but didn't mention it. "Don't worry, I'm not here about the Mutilator incident. But I do have a few questions relating to it."

"Of course, anything for our nation's best boys and gals in blue."

"Has anyone been asking about having another suit made?"

"Our research and dev team was contacted by an anonymous buyer about it, but after the Phineas Crane incident we refused to sell to anyone else."

"What about before?"

"No. It was all Mr. Crane's idea. We designed it and offered to manufacture a whole series of them at a fraction of the initial cost, but he only ordered the one. Cheap bastard. But the only copies of the blueprints are in our archives and the ones your division confiscated from Crane."

"And who has access to your archives?"

"Our archives are available for public viewing, though are managed by a select few, myself included. I can give you their names if you like."

"Could somebody have created a copy of the plans?"

"Not unless they drew them out by hand. All Star Five blueprints are equipped with anti-electronic reproduction measures."

"Even the one Crane had?"

"He might have had it removed. When a client pays for the blueprints, they're free to do what they like with them."

"I see."

"Wait a minute," Changi said, eyes widening. "Does this mean there's *another* police-killing psycho out there in one of our suits?"

Miller groaned inwardly, He'd probably revealed too much. This was a federal matter after all. He tried a laugh. "Let's just call it a precaution."

Changi handed Miller a data card. "These are my contact details. If you can't get the blueprints out of evidence, contact me and I'll send you a copy. If there is a new suit, I want it on record that Star Five Enterprises had nothing to do with it."

"Then who did?"

"My best guess would be AkanneCorp, though you'd never prove it. They'd bastardize our design and cut corners, but there'd be similar enough features. You might be able to figure something out from the blueprints.

Miller nodded. "Thank you."

●———————————————●

Crane was enjoying himself immensely. He admired Miller, but the sergeant was hardly a renaissance man. These people, however, appreciated the differences between Stravinsky and Tchaikovsky, Monet and Afremov, Bordeaux and Margaux. His kind of people.

He intercepted the first waiter he came across, sampling one of the balsamic-glazed peach and prosciutto canapes from his tray. After subsisting on beige prison swill for the past year, it was a veritable explosion of flavor in his mouth. Next, he helped himself to a glass of some new hybrid liquor he couldn't identify. It was far too bitter for his palate, but he didn't care.

Collins had disappeared, probably to pump himself full of Stimz in the bathroom. He briefly entertained the thought of making a getaway, but he was tired and ill-equipped to deal with the additional police patrols. Besides, his pride wouldn't let him leave.

Even as he soaked up the atmosphere, his eyes constantly scanned the room, taking in a multitude of tiny details. If Lady Luck deigned to smile on them, the imposter may well be present. Over two dozen individuals matched the height Dr. Shields had given to Miller. Of those, less than half had a physique that could possibly fit into the suit, and only two of *those* carried themselves like they could fight, let alone kill a federal agent.

Before long, he found himself enthralling a handful of other guests with an entirely fabricated anecdote involving a brush with an incognito Russian president.

"…and that's the secret to the best Borscht I have ever tasted!" he said, and everybody laughed.

One laugh grew closer until a hand came down on his shoulder. "Layton, you old rogue!"

Crane's immediate instinct was to grab the hand and break it, but remembering he was in polite company, he turned around, smiling. "Hello, Charles!"

It was a lucky guess. The billionaire guffawed, then recoiled in mock-horror. "My goodness, man, what happened to you?"

Crane twisted his mouth into a grimace. "That's the last time I get work done in Detroit."

"I hope you're planning to sue them stupid."

"I'll put the wheels in motion while I'm recovering from the shock in the Bahamas."

"Good man! Feel free to use my legal team." Danton gestured around at their surroundings. "What do you think of my little shindig?"

"Fantastic, Charles. You've outdone yourself."

Danton frowned. "It's not as big as last year."

"Yes," said Crane without missing a beat, "but there's something to be said for an understated affair."

Danton smiled again. "You're right!"

"I gotta ask you something, Charles," Crane said, deftly steering the conversation elsewhere. "What's with the gray-eyed guys?"

"Mars Group mercenaries," said Danton. "They're here at the request of my surprise guest."

No sooner had he said this, his watch beeped. "Speaking of, he's just arrived. Excuse me, Layton, I must go meet him." Danton ducked away.

Crane searched around for the waiter with the delightful canapes and found Miller instead.

"Where's Nichols?" he asked.

"I don't know."

Before Miller could answer, Danton stopped the band and took to the stage, calling for everyone's attention. "Ladies and gentlemen, thank you all for being here tonight. Otherwise, I would have bought this tux for nothing and have to drink all this booze myself!"

Crane laughed along with the other guests. Miller looked like he was forcing his.

Danton worked the room for a few minutes, good-naturedly ribbing a few of his more prominent guests. If DuroCorp ever folded, he could eke out a modest living as a jobbing comedian.

Then, the billionaire revealed the ace up his sleeve—the guest of honor, martial-artist turned silver screen action superstar Chad Savage.

Miller watched as a ripple of excited murmurs ran through the crowd. Though he had a net worth of one hundred and eighty million—pocket change for some of the guests—there was something of the glitz, glamour and scandal of Tinseltown reflected in him that appealed to their baser natures. Taut, trim, tan, with perfect teeth and sun-bleached hair, Savage epitomized Hollywood handsome, with charisma to spare.

Last year had marked his first foray into drama with *Villas of Mars*. Rumor had it he was in line for a Golden Apollo award.

"We designed his auditory filters."

Miller almost jumped. He hadn't heard Lin Changi sidle up beside him. He glanced to where Crane had stood, but he'd gone.

"Auditory filters?" He was stalling for time as he looked.

"Chad Savage does his own stunts, which invariably involve walking away from explosions. Some studios still prefer using actual explosives, which they then enhance with computer graphics. But what about the noise?"

She didn't let Miller reply.

"So we created the filters. They're surgically embedded in his ear canal, unobtrusive, but they automatically seal themselves when they register any noise approaching a hundred decibels, protecting his hearing. Cool, huh? So the ungrateful bastard drops us as sponsors and signs on with AkanneCorp."

Miller made note of the second mention of AkanneCorp. Another possible lead if nothing else came from the evening.

He looked around, noticing the other guests moving outside.

"What's going on?" Changi asked a nearby woman.

"Chad Savage brought his stunt team. He's gonna give us a demonstration."

Out in the courtyard, a series of crash mats had been set up in a giant square pattern. Figures clad in black ninja uniforms emblazoned with an AkanneCorp logo and CS Stunt Crew across their backs stood on each side and corner.

Chad removed his jacket, tie and shirt, earning him appreciative applause from the crowd. Kicking off his shoes, he handed the pile one of the Mars Group mercs, then stepped onto the mat.

Hopping lightly from foot to foot, he moved into the center and executed a few warm-up kicks.

At an unseen signal, the figures on the outside converged on his position and, one by one, he took them all down. Though no contact was made, the stunt crew sold each hit, until the last one took a flying kick to an obviously padded torso and fell out of the square.

The crowd applauded again and Savage bowed. The mercenary tossed him a towel and a bottle of antiperspirant, then handed over each item of clothing as Savage changed, finishing it all with a spritz of cologne. The movie star joined the crowd amid smiles, handshakes and pecks on the cheek from blushing guests, male and female.

Miller hung back. Though this time it was purely for show, there was no mistaking the fighting style—flashy, with a lot of unnecessary jumping, spinning and yelling. A unique hybrid style almost identical to the one he'd seen in the surveillance footage of the copycat killer.

CHAPTER 16

Managing to shake Changi, Miller went to find Crane. He stood with Agent Nichols over by the food table.

"Savage is the killer," Crane insisted.

"That's ridiculous," said Nichols. "He's an actor, not an assassin."

"Yes, but his power armor gives him the edge. He's rich enough to afford a suit of his own, and he could have had Norwich killed and taken the blueprints for himself. Who'd suspect one of the country's most recognizable men?"

"Do you have any idea how stupid this sounds?" Nichols asked.

Miller nearly agreed. It seemed a stretch to suddenly happen across the perpetrator. But every so often, the stars of coincidence and convenience aligned to reveal an answer.

Or else, it was a setup and the real perpetrator was pulling unseen strings to throw them off the trail.

"What proof do you have?" continued Nichols.

"When you have my experience, you learn to read other fighters," said Crane. "They all have their own styles, idiosyncrasies, strengths and weaknesses. Savage's style matches that of the killer in the footage you showed us, albeit slower without the suit. The same agility, the same flourishes and spinning kicks. Isn't that right, Miller?"

"It's very similar." Miller looked to make sure nobody was listening.

"It's not enough to go on," said Nichols.

"Then beat a bloody confession out of him, if you must, I don't care! I promised you the killer's identity and have subsequently delivered. What happens next is up to you."

"If we arrest him and we're wrong, do you know what it would do to the department?"

"Careful, Gregory. It sounds like the bureau's reputation is more important to you than the lives of its agents," said Crane.

Nichols grabbed a cracker spread with pate and shoved it into his mouth, ending the conversation. Miller rolled his eyes, hardly believing this sort of man was entrusted with national security.

Collins returned, making an effort to avoid eye contact. No doubt he'd been getting his Stimz fix. With Nichols distracted by the food, Miller noticed Crane slip into the crowd, and Collins followed.

Crane angled toward the movie star. He wanted to try eavesdropping. As he drew closer, though, the mercenary from the demonstration – 'Adam' according to his name tag- appeared next to Savage and whispered something before leading him away. Although too far away to hear, Crane knew what had been said.

With little else to do while incarcerated, between feeding, chess matches and beatings, he had taught himself to read lips, watching the men guarding his cube as they chatted idly. Adam had said only three words—*Sweetman is compromised.*

Savage now knew the substitute had been uncovered. Of course, if he was behind the murders, it followed he'd been the one to organize the killing of Norwich in the first place. In fact, Singleton's description of the man from the apartment could easily apply to several Mars Group mercenaries. None of them had the surgical scar, however, though there were ways of concealing such markings.

If they'd been responsible for Norwich's death, they would know something was amiss the second they laid eyes on the disguised Crane.

He stepped behind a waiter, keeping his face away from Savage, knowing he may already be too late. To his left, he glimpsed the nearest mercenary break into a steady walk toward him.

Crane didn't fancy his chances of subduing the man. Keeping himself fit during his imprisonment had been one thing, but he hadn't fought anyone in over a year, in or out of his power suit, and he was probably rusty. In any case, he couldn't risk making a scene and scaring off Savage. Or perhaps he *should* make a scene.

Crane surreptitiously stuck out a foot, tripping the closest waiter. Glassware smashed on the ground, causing nearby partygoers to shriek and exclaim while two more waiters and one of the regular guards came over to help. Crane melted back into the crowd, keeping his head down.

He let Collins catch up to him, Miller close behind, though once again, he couldn't see Nichols. "We've been rumbled."

"I can't get hold of the DCMP teams," Miller said. "I think we're being jammed."

Even Collins seemed to understand the trouble they were in. He looked over Crane's shoulder. "Mars Group at three and nine o'clock."

Crane didn't need to verify. "I think it's time to regroup. Out through the kitchen."

Miller felt his left hand clench into a fist. Unable to contact the DCMP and with Agent Nichols nowhere to be found, the three men were on their own. A convicted serial killer and a drug-addicted security contractor weren't his first choice of allies, either.

They were outnumbered, and with no union to regulate them, the Mars Group mercenaries likely had no qualms about killing.

They weren't the only ones trying to escape through the kitchen.

Flanked by three Mars Group mercs, Savage grinned back at them from the other side. "I see you guys got my invitation. If you make it out of here, I'll be in touch."

He turned to the mercenaries. "Fellas, try not to kill them, okay?"

Savage slipped out the exit with Adam, leaving two mercenaries with nametags reading "Frank" and "Steve." Glancing back, Miller spotted two more behind, cutting off their retreat, and loosened his collar, preparing for a fistfight.

"I bloody knew it," said Crane. "No chance you chaps want to sort this out civilly?"

"Hell with it," Collins declared, removing his jacket and tie, flinging them aside, then charging at the pair in front.

The one named Frank rushed to engage him. Stimz met Burnout as they collided with the force of professional linebackers.

Miller didn't have time to watch beyond the initial impact. Settling into a comfortable low-hand-guard stance, he waited for Steve to make the first move. A predictable left feint was followed by a right hook, which Miller ducked to avoid. He was glad his reflexes were holding up. Had it connected, the blow would have been devastating.

Miller was trained as a counterpuncher, always watching for an opponent's mistake. When a wild swing left Steve open, he took his chance. Jabbing twice below the ribs with his right hand, he landed a hook with his left, another with his right, ending the combo with an elbow strike up under the chin.

Each hit was precise, but the cranked-up mercenary was unfazed. Miller needed more power. The cop shuffled back just in time to avoid a knee, but instead of lowering his leg back to the ground, Steve extended his foot into a round-house kick. At the last second, Miller managed to parry with his right arm, grunting with the impact.

As a boxer, he'd rarely had use for kicking, and should have realized his opponent would have no such restriction. He adapted, shifting to a high-guard and closing the distance, giving Steve no room to kick again. The mercenary fired out with a cross, which Miller absorbed with his arm, dropping his elbow as Steve tried for a body shot.

Coming up under his guard, Miller let loose with an uppercut, but Steve was waiting for this. Rolling with the punch, he stepped forward again to envelop Miller in a crushing bear hug, then hurled him to the ground. Though Miller managed to protect his head, his landing drove the wind out of him. Gasping for air, he felt himself being lifted up and flung into the nearby bench.

He struggled to his feet, but Steve had him by the throat. Before he knew it, he was pinned down against the stovetop, mere inches from the heating element. Desperate, he tried to hit back, but the blow glanced off the other man's shoulder.

Even as the grip tightened around his throat, Miller's eyes wandered over to where Collins was brawling with his mercenary.

No help there.

A metallic flash brought Miller back, and he realized Steve had grabbed a knife. He tried breaking the grip on his neck with his left hand as he pushed against the knife-arm with his right. In his peripheral, he saw the heavy-looking pan on the stove next to him. Letting go with his left, he gripped the side of it, trying to ignore the blistering pain, and swung up.

As the pan crashed into the side of his head, Steve released Miller, who shoved him back.

By the time he stood, the heat was too much and he dropped the pan, but Steve managed to retain the knife. The mercenary switched to a forward grip and lunged. Miller's response was pure reflex, grabbing the arm with both hands and redirecting the blade, forcing it backward.

It took him a few seconds to realize why the mercenary had shuddered to a stop. Looking down, Miller saw the knife lodged just below the man's sternum. He let go, and Steve collapsed to the ground, twitching as shock fought Burnout for control of his body.

Breathing raggedly, Miller looked around at the others.

Crane, now sans his prosthetic arm, was rolling one of the other mercenaries into the recovery position. A second lay unconscious nearby. Miller hadn't even seen the Englishman take them down.

Collins had his opponent immobilized against the wall, arms bent up behind his back.

Crane looked over to him and saw Steve on the ground. "What happened to 'try not to kill anybody?'"

CHAPTER 17

While Collins went out to alert the DCMP patrols, Miller used a tea towel to try to stem the flow of blood from the wounded mercenary.

Crane sat cross-legged nearby, observing him intently.

"Why aren't you escaping?" Miller asked without looking up.

"Chalk it up to unfinished business."

Miller kept up the pressure until a pair of DCMP officers burst in, blasters at the ready. One of them rang for an ambulance, then took over from the exhausted Miller, while the other kept Crane covered.

The Mutilator sat perfectly still, arm behind his head. His prosthetic forearm was recovered and reattached before he was put in a pair of restraints again.

A lieutenant arrived and Miller explained the situation. The bruising on his neck collaborated his claim of self-defense, and the incapacitated mercenaries were led away.

Miller didn't mention that Savage was their prime suspect. After all, without concrete proof, why would they believe him? The DCMP wouldn't want to risk their own reputation if such a high-profile case was thrown out due to a lack of evidence.

It would have been nice if the man had lent them a few officers to help watch over Crane, but apparently, the DCMP had washed their hands of that matter too.

"We're safer than them anyway," said Collins. "Crane's got some kind of crush on you, and I'm not even a cop."

"Charming," muttered Crane, who'd been well within earshot.

Back in the limo, Crane, Collins and Miller discussed the night's events.

The idea of a movie star being responsible for murdering federal agents still seemed incongruous. But the more Miller thought about it, the more Savage fit the bill—right-handed, athletic, with a background in martial arts. He looked a little shorter than five foot eleven—the height Dr. Shields described—but the suit could have easily been modified to add an extra inch. Plus, what he'd said to them seemed to indicate he *was* the one they were after.

"If only we had hard evidence," said Crane, rubbing at his Semblatex with a rag soaked in an alcohol-based solvent.

There was also the issue of Agent Nichols. Perhaps if he'd stuck around, the DCMP would have been more cooperative.

As if on cue, Miller's phone rang. It was Nichols. "Where the hell have you been?" he asked, activating the speaker function.

"Shut up and listen, Sergeant," Nichols said. He sounded frightened. *"I was out getting some fresh air when I saw Savage being hurried out to his car. I thought it was suspicious after what you said, so I followed them."*

The agent gave him an address, which Singleton put into the limo's nav computer.

"And hurry up. They're heading back to Los Angeles… oh God… they've spotted me!"

Someone shouted. Miller heard Nichols breaking into a run.

"For God's sake, get over he—" and the line went dead.

"Step on it, Singleton," Crane said. "It's time to end a superstar's career!"

* * *

The address Nichols had given them was a hotel almost as extravagant as the Regal Grande.

Singleton was sent in to gather intel. Posing as a producer wanting to meet Savage on behalf of an indie filmmaker, he convinced the woman at the front desk to divulge where he was. Naturally, he had the penthouse suite.

Singleton waited in the car while Crane, Collins and Miller went around the back of the hotel. Using the override code, Miller unlocked the door, leading them inside, undetected.

Avoiding the cameras, they took the stairs up twenty flights. Fatigued mentally and physically, Miller powered on after Collins and Crane, determined not to be the weak link and praying their quarry was still there.

Reaching the top floor, they stopped, allowing him to catch his breath while they discussed their plan of attack. They decided hitting hard and fast was the best approach.

Collins took point, kicking in the door, Miller close behind.

Two Mars Group mercs whirled around too late, both taken out by stun shots. Half-dressed, Savage was looking out the enormous window at the city below, martini in hand.

"Police!" said Miller. "Put your hands up and turn around slowly."

As instructed, the actor raised his hands and turned, dropping the glass as he did so.

"Phineas Crane," he said, flashing a smile. "I'd wondered who the fed contacted. You know, he *actually* wiped his phone when my guys caught him? I thought they only did that in the movies!"

Adam emerged from the kitchen, carrying a tray of food for his employer, stopping short when he saw Miller aiming at him. Carefully placing the tray on the table, he put his hands behind his head.

"You too, Savage," said Collins. "Hands behind your head now."

Still grinning, Savage complied.

Crane, meanwhile, had spotted a storage trunk. "Bloody hell, don't tell me your suit's in there."

"Alright." Savage chuckled. "It's not in there."

Crane shook his head in disbelief. "You know, I rather hoped my impersonator would display a little more intelligence."

Savage shrugged.

Miller was just glad their little sting operation had gone off so well. Still, all that remained was to restrain them, call for backup, find Nichols, and hand Savage over to the FBI. Simple.

"Sorry about this, Adam," the actor said to his employee.

Acute pain assailed Miller and he dropped to the ground, clutching at his ears. Adam, Collins and Crane were also writhing in pain. It was some sort of ultrasonic weapon.

Savage looked completely unbothered even as webbed cracks appeared in the DuroGlass behind him, and Miller remembered the auditory filters Star Five Enterprises had developed for him.

Then, as suddenly as it hit, the pain faded, but his ears still rang and the room still spun.

Savage took his hands down and waggled the signet ring on his left hand at them. "Pretty cool, huh? You know, I'm impressed, Crane. You bested my boys and tracked me down a lot quicker than I anticipated. But it ain't time for the grand finale yet."

Miller watched as Crane pushed himself to his feet with some effort. The Mutilator didn't waste time with pithy retorts, but vaulted over the sofa, taking the fight to Savage.

But no matter how fast Crane struck, Savage moved faster, ducking and weaving, pivoting and twisting, close yet infuriatingly far.

As they fought, Miller could see that Savage was maneuvering Crane closer and closer to the window. He tried to shout a warning, but Savage jumped, kicking Crane squarely in the chest.

Crane crashed into the weakened DuroGlass, which cracked yet still managed to hold. He sank to the ground, stunned.

Miller recovered enough to clamber to his feet and charged, but Savage kicked him in the injured knee, which gave way beneath him. Savage slammed a palm into the hinge of his jaw, and Miller hit the floor again.

Adam had also shaken off the worst of the effects, drawing his own sidearm to shoot Collins.

"Don't shoot," said Savage, making toward the door, carefully avoiding the broken martini glass shards. He gestured at the trunk. "Help me."

Fuming, the employee holstered his weapon and picked up the other end of the cumbersome trunk, hauling it out to the elevator. "What about the others?"

"They were dumb enough to get captured. Leave 'em."

Adam shrugged.

By the time Miller struggled back up again and limped out after them, the doors had slid closed and they were gone. At first, he couldn't believe they'd been beaten so badly. But at the same time, he shouldn't have been surprised. They'd gone in with no backup, minimal preparation and still fatigued from the fight at Butler Parkes. He had no clue what they'd do now, especially with Agent Nichols gone.

Miller went back, ignoring a groaning Collins and picked up his blaster, leveling it at Crane. "You good?"

The Mutilator rubbed at the back of his head. "Nothing damaged but my ego. Savage?"

"Gone."

Probing at a loose molar with his tongue, Miller considered the Mutilator, vulnerable and unarmed. If he decided to shoot the killer there and then, nobody could stop him. The satellites would register his shot, but it wouldn't be hard to convince the higher-ups he'd simply fired in self-defense.

But even if he could get away with it, he didn't feel like dealing with the guilt. Less over the death of Crane, he felt that was long-deserved, but he knew the specter of Marion wouldn't let him forget what he'd done.

Besides, something the Mutilator had said had been niggling at the back of his mind.

He lowered the blaster, but kept it at the ready.

"Ah, good old altruism," Crane said.

"Shooting's too good for you," he retorted.

"How considerate."

"Yesterday, you said you only killed crooked cops.".

"In a nutshell."

"Yet you killed Vic. My partner, who I trusted with my life."

"Then I'm afraid your trust was misplaced," Crane said, simply. "Among other things, Sergeant Baxter was my informant. That's how I was ready for you that night when you raided my hideout."

Anger bubbled up inside him, tempered only by fatigue. "You're wrong," he growled.

"Your belief changes nothing. I do not make a decision to take another life lightly. I research, I investigate, I dig for dirt. If I determine an officer of the law to be corrupt, I then take matters into my own hands."

"And what gives you the right to decide?"

"Every bribe taken. Every illicit narcotic used. Every scrap of evidence missing or fabricated. Every innocent civilian caught in the crossfire. Every instance of excessive force, brutality or profiling. Every blind eye. Every betrayal of the public your colleagues have sworn to safeguard. They place their trust in the thin blue line and, for too long, that trust has been violated again and again. That, Sergeant, is what gives me the right."

While Crane spoke with authority, not once did he raise his voice. Clearly, he'd given a lot of thought to the matter. It didn't excuse his actions by any means.

Nevertheless, Miller was reminded of all the times Vic had disappeared without explanation. Giving his trusted partner benefit of the doubt, he had chalked his behavior up to personal reasons and never pressed the issue.

"It wasn't just Baxter," continued Crane. "The entire team mired themselves in filth—Graf, Winslow, Smith, Easterbrook, Ramsey. Every one of them, rotten to the core. You weren't supposed to be there that night."

That, Miller supposed, was true. Vic had wanted to go without him, but Miller would not be dissuaded.

Collins lumbered over before they could discuss it further. "Anyone wanna explain how the hell we just lost?"

"Savage played us," said Miller. "Even with the element of surprise, we were outclassed."

"I didn't expect him to be so fast, even without the suit," said Crane. "He must have been holding back at the party."

"You think he's enhanced?"

"At that speed, he'd have to be. Altikinetic reflexes would be my guess."

"How do you fight that?"

Crane smiled wanly and tapped the side of his head. "Psychology." He was adept at that.

There was a knock at the door. Singleton was the only one who knew they were there, but he would have called first if he was coming up.

Collins aimed his blaster at the door as Miller opened it. Standing there was a man and a woman in suits similar to Agent Nichols. The woman was carrying an FBI badge.

"Gentlemen," she said. "Special Agent Webber. I assume you're the ones Agent Nichols roped into his investigation?"

Miller nodded.

"Our computers picked up an emergency signal from his phone when it got wiped and this was the last known location. Do you know where he is?"

Miller gave a shortened version of their investigation. Special Agent Webber looked understandably incredulous. "The *actor*."

"He's the killer you're looking for," Crane said. "Find him and you'll find Agent Nichols."

"Do you have proof?"

"He attacked us!" Collins said.

"You burst in and zapped his bodyguards. Legally, he can claim self-defense. I don't know about the BMPD, but we have enough problems already without a defamation case from one of the biggest stars in Hollywood. We'll take what you've told us under advisement, but until we have concrete evidence, then as far as the FBI is concerned, Chad Savage is innocent. In the meantime, I suggest the three of you return home before you get arrested for interfering in a federal case."

Webber called ahead to organize the tiltrotor to take them back to Baltimore, then sent them on their way.

"So what the hell do we do now?" asked Collins as they left the room. "Just let him go free?"

"Of course not," said Crane. "He said the grand finale was yet to come. If we wait, he'll come to us."

———————•

They took one final trip to the hotel to change out of their bloodied tuxedos, then went back to Reagan National.

Once in the air, Miller settled back into his seat and closed his eyes. The scarring on his hand itched again, but he ignored it. Though his body begged for sleep, his mind was too restless, thinking about how close he'd come to dying in the past few days. He wished he could go home and argue with Marion about taking unnecessary risks.

Then there was the stabbing. He knew he should feel bad about potentially taking another life, but he didn't. It had been self-defense. Just like Brick at the Hippodrome. As far as they were concerned, his conscience was clear. Not getting to bring Savage to justice was disappointing, but the sun would rise tomorrow regardless. He'd be back on patrol or responding to a domestic disturbance.

I can't go on. I'll go on.

A relaxed Collins sat a few rows ahead. If he felt any remorse over nearly killing Miller, he didn't show it.

Crane sat across from him, manacled again, picking off Semblatex with his fingers and staring out the window. Miller guessed he was brooding over his imposter. Losing to him must have been a crushing blow to the Mutilator's ego. Just like, he assumed, when he'd first arrested Crane.

CHAPTER 18

Baltimore—One Year Before

Phineas Crane sat comfortably before a bank of computer monitors. Half a dozen screens cycled through live feeds of the various cameras hidden throughout the block of flats. Each room was fully furnished, but only his was occupied. Ideally, his impending guests wouldn't realize this until it was too late.

As he waited, he flexed the fingers of his cybernetic left hand. Four years on, he was *still* getting used to the sensation.

Movement caught his eye and he turned his focus to the top right screen. Outside, two vans pulled up to the curb. The vehicles were unmarked, but he knew they were BMPD. They were here for him, after all. Eight police officers murdered over the course of two years was bound to attract their attention. The Metro Mutilator had been quiet the past eleven months or so, but he was far from finished.

This would be his magnum opus. Twelve in one attack. He would send a message, both to the public and law enforcement throughout the country.

The police filed out of the vans and peeled off into two squads; a typical tactical strike. He watched as one squad hurried to the front door, while the others moved through the side alley around to the back.

Crane smiled at their haste. They should have had people cordoning off the road, or at least some shield generators. He was surprised they weren't fast-roping down from a helicopter. But he'd been counting on their rushing.

Little over an hour earlier, an informant had divulged his whereabouts to the police over at the first precinct. After verifying this with a photo, the BMPD sprang into action. They hadn't forgotten what he'd done to their own and weren't about to let him slip through their fingers again. Though helmets obscured their faces, he knew their names, their faces and, most importantly, their sins.

Sylvia Easterbrook, who'd misappropriated narcotics from the evidence room. Eric Graf, who'd strong-armed money from petty criminals. John Winslow, who'd accepted bribes from wealthier arrestees, then deleted the records. Lesley Smith, who'd killed a whistle-blower on behalf of a pharmaceuticals conglomerate.

Crane quelled a flash of excitement as they opened the doors with their public override code, entering through both the front and rear of the building.

Then he saw something that gave him pause. He recognized the blue mackintosh and battered homburg hat of Sergeant Myles Miller, leading the second team.

Crane frowned. Miller wasn't meant to be there. The others were crooked, corrupt, rotten through and through. They needed to die. But Miller was honest. To kill him would detract from his statement.

What could he do? He could always abort, still having plenty of time to escape, but he'd been planning this for far too long to throw it all away now. He'd adapt. He always did.

He reached over and pushed a button on the console, dropping the shutters over all entrances. Made of DuroSteel and reinforced with reflective titanium and ceramic-carbonate alloy, they were impervious to blaster fire. He could imagine panic creeping into their DigiComm transmissions. Any moment now, someone would try calling for backup, but their long-range comm signals wouldn't get through, thanks to the jamming devices he'd had installed throughout the building.

It hadn't come cheap, but his unwitting benefactor had money to spare.

Years earlier, he'd tracked down one Layton Norwich and foiled an attempt on his life. Crane himself had coerced a junkie to attack the multi-millionaire while he was traveling incognito one day. Promised five hundred standard, the hapless conspirator had received a sound beating and ten years' imprisonment instead.

Crane, on the other hand, had gained the perfect toehold into the good books of Norwich. He milked the goodwill for all it was worth, persuading him to fund his cybernetic replacement hand, the development of his power armor and the revamping of the flats. If the multi-millionaire ever voiced his concerns about the expenditures, Crane convinced him they were necessary.

Both teams cautiously advanced. They had no other choice.

Standing, he moved to where his mechanized suit waited, mounted on its rack. Flipping the activation switch, he stepped onto the footplate and spread his arms against the rack. Piece by piece, the armor enclosed around him. Torso first, feet and legs, and arms. Finally, he took the helmet hanging next to him, put it on and tested the built-in camera.

Stepping down, he picked up the last components from the nearby workbench. First, he slipped a micro-console over his left wrist, which would allow him to wirelessly control certain functions in the building; another gift from Norwich. Next, he put on a set of metallic claws, which the fingers of his artificial hand slotted into. The claws were comprised of monomolecular-bonded steel, which could cut through armor. He flexed the fingers again experimentally. As an afterthought, he clipped on a holster, into which he inserted a neuro disruption weapon.

Cutting the lights, he went out to meet his guests.

On the levels below, the strike-teams were plunged into darkness. At an order from Baxter, they all switched on the night-vision function in their helmet visors. All except Miller, who wore no helmet, using a flashlight instead.

As they made their way up the first flight of stairs, he knew Sergeant Baxter would lead his team from room to room on the ground floor, looking for one that wasn't shuttered.

"He knows," somebody said over the DigiComms. *"It's a damn trap!"*

"Cool it," hissed Baxter. *"We still outnumber him. Everybody put your breathers on just in case."*

The cops donned their respirators one at a time, while their teammates kept watch.

Miller spoke up. "He may have electrified certain areas. Your insulated soles should protect you, but to be safe, don't touch any walls."

He didn't like the situation in the least. With minimal intel, they had no idea what lay in wait for them. How many civilians were in the area? Was the Mutilator alone? Was he even there?

But Baxter, showing unusual impulsiveness, had insisted that it was now or never, and Miller would be damned if he'd let his best friend on the force walk into the lion's den without him.

"Eyes open, people," Baxter said. *"We're ending this bastard tonight! Lethal force is authorized. Shoot to kill."*

On the middle floor, Crane waited around the corner as the second team approached, watching them via the camera in the hall, which transmitted a live feed to the micro-console on his wrist. Miller had taken the lead, making it easier for him to deal with him first.

Waiting until the sergeant was almost within reach, he touched the screen, opening a door behind them. Predictably, the antsy officers spun in the direction of the sound.

Darting forward, he drew and activated the neuro disruptor, pressing it to the side of Miller's neck. The weapon sent an electrosonic pulse through his body, targeting the synapses and knocking him unconscious. Crane caught him as he collapsed, dragging him back around the corner, then sealed off the hallway.

He dragged Miller into the nearest room. A former storage space, the room was now empty but for an old mattress, and a lone steel manacle bolted to the wall. Crane had installed it himself. Low-tech, but efficient.

He placed the sergeant onto the mattress and shackled his arm to the wall. Now Miller was out of harm's way.

Heading back to the corridor, he could hear the other police shouting frantically to each other.

Through the security feed, he watched them in the dark, pulse rifles whipping back and forth in panic.

Touching the console again, Crane turned the hall lights on full. The abrupt shift in brightness, amplified by their night vision, disoriented them. Music began blaring from wall-mounted speakers, adding to the confusion as the corridor re-opened.

Then Crane was among them.

Though it was hardly professional, he found himself imagining the horror of the team downstairs as they heard their teammates being slaughtered over their DigiComms, backed by a wailing blues track. Even in his old life, he'd always had an affinity for the old blues legends, and the John Lee Hooker number seemed oddly appropriate.

The last officer fell, and Crane appropriated a DigiComm as he hid again.

"Upstairs now!" he heard Baxter shouting, straining to be heard. *"Weapons free, go, go, go! And somebody cut the damn music!"*

Two officers targeted the nearest speakers and took them out, but the music still played throughout the building.

"Light up anything that moves," ordered Baxter. *"Mid-range shots, people."*

As Officer Winslow rounded the corner, Crane snatched him out of the hall and shoved him into the nearest room. Snapping the officer's neck, Crane dropped him to the ground and remerged into the hall.

He emerged from the doorway and they opened fire. Theoretically, if they concentrated their fire, they could overload the superconductive properties of his suit. He wouldn't give them the chance.

Mechanized legs launched him across the hall, ramming into Smith like a pile-driver. Easterbrook shifted aim and fired higher, and Crane brought up his right arm so the dispersive plating afforded his head extra protection as he closed in, then slashed out with the claws. They cleanly sliced through both DuroPlas barrel and a good deal of circuitry. Knocking the useless gun from Easterbrook's grasp, Crane stepped forward and sliced the officer's throat on the backswing.

As Smith fought to stand, Crane dropped to a knee, down on his level, and punched him directly in the trachea, crushing his windpipe. This left Baxter and Officer Ramsey.

Crane swept up Easterbrook's pulse rifle. Ramsey pulled the trigger again and again, but Crane rose under his line of fire, swinging the gun. The rifle butt slammed into the cop, cracking his visor.

Ducking, Crane swung again, catching Ramsey in the knee, then kicked his legs out from under him. As the cop hit the ground, he trapped him under one knee, then stabbed him in the neck.

Looking up, he was mildly surprised to see Baxter had not fled. The sergeant stood firm, pulse rifle steady, staring the Mutilator down.

Maybe he could get the sergeant talking. He checked his wrist interface to make sure his cam helmet was still recording.

"What have you done with Miller?" Baxter asked.

Crane was taken aback.

"What's this?" he asked, vocal filters disguising his voice. "A glimmer of selflessness?"

"Where. Is. He?"

"Subdued, but otherwise unharmed."

"Let him go," said Baxter. "Come on, eleven out of twelve ain't bad. I didn't even want him here in the first place."

"Don't worry, Baxter, he'll walk away unscathed. Unfortunately, the same can't be said for you."

"Hurry up, then," said Baxter. "I don't have all night."

Crane chuckled. "Not just yet. I couldn't let you go without first expressing my gratitude."

"For what?" His eyes narrowed.

"Tonight is about two things. The first is sending a message. Abuse of authority by the BMPD will no longer be tolerated. The second is to redress the imbalance of the lawful and the unlawful among your ranks. Without your generous contribution, my efforts would have been far more painstaking."

"My contribution?"

"Your files," Crane said. "Extensive records on more than fifty officers, detailing their many transgressions, or lack thereof, in far too few instances. Presumably blackmail material, in case any of your fellow rats turn on you."

Baxter frowned. "How did you—"

"You are most forthcoming with total strangers you meet in a bar, myself included."

"I *gave* you the files?"

Crane shook his head. "No, only access to them. In your defense, you wouldn't recognize me out of this suit, and you *were* highly inebriated."

"You gotta be kidding," Baxter muttered, more to himself than anyone.

"Naturally, you neglected to include yourself in the files, so I had to make do with my own research. Not as commendably thorough as yours, but I did find some interesting titbits. Fancy framing poor Officer Nassos simply because she rejected your advances!"

"Don't you judge me! At least *I* haven't killed anyone."

As they spoke, Baxter edged his way back along the wall, ever so slowly. Crane let him. He knew there wasn't anywhere for the sergeant to go. If he wanted to play cat-and-mouse, so be it. "No, you haven't. You just settled for ruining the career of an honest, hardworking woman. Did you know she's tried to take her own life three times since then?"

Baxter said nothing.

"Interesting how a number of those corrupt officers happened to turn up tonight," he continued, changing the subject. "Twelve, had Miller not invited himself along. In place of Jed Bouchard, I'd wager. Why is that, I wonder?"

"You're so smart, you tell me."

Further and further Baxter inched.

"My guess is they knew about your files," Crane said, thoughtfully. "You intimated that you've arranged for their dirty little secrets to go public if anything happened to you."

Now it was Baxter's turn to laugh. "No wonder you've always been two steps ahead of us. But why go to all the trouble of killing us when you could expose us all yourself?"

"And risk you covering it up? Not bloody likely. The consequences of your actions must be seen. But now, I think that's quite enough stalling, don't you? It's time to pay the proverbial piper now, Victor."

Instead of resisting, Baxter dropped his rifle and removed his helmet. He looked tired. "Alright then. But you have to look me in the eyes while you do it."

"Makes no difference to me," said Crane, moving forward.

Before he could reach the officer, Baxter threw his helmet at him. Reflexively, he caught the headgear, giving the officer the chance to make his move. It wasn't the corner he'd been making for, but the fire alarm switch on the wall. He pulled the switch, setting off the siren and activating the CO2 suppressors.

It was a smart delaying tactic. The system dispersed a fine powder chemically treated to absorb fuel, which obscured Crane's vision and made his footing more precarious. It wasn't enough to deter him. He caught up within a few strides, and struck out, claws piercing Baxter's armor and stabbing into his spinal cord.

With a gasp, Vic Baxter sank to the ground. Crane observed his handiwork with a slight sense of satisfaction.

As he made his way over to shut off the alarm, he heard rapid footsteps approaching. He turned as a figure, obscured by a haze of powder particles, swung something heavy-looking at him.

At the last second, he raised his bionic arm, warding off the blow. Even so, the impact was greater than he anticipated and he almost lost balance.

The assailant stepped forward, revealing the face of Officer Graf.

You bloody idiot! Crane thought to himself in dismay. *Focus!*

Eric Graf was the most problematic of the strike team. Officially, he was just another cop, but per Baxter's files, he was surgically enhanced. Graf kept this quiet to avoid the intense scrutiny enhanced police often received. He could manipulate his endocrinal system, triggering a temporary burst of super-human strength, heightened speed and increased endurance.

Crane couldn't believe he'd forgotten that, preoccupied while toying with Baxter. The sergeant must have been stall-ing, waiting for the enhanced cop to make a move.

Apparently, Graf had seen an opportunity to get Baxter out of his hair, regardless of the files going public. Either way, Crane had a real fight on his hands. With his suit, he stood a good chance against Graf, but he'd allowed himself to become distracted.

As it was, the suppressing powder over his visor was making it increasingly harder to see. For the first time that night, he felt a jolt of apprehension. Graf swung again, and he barely managed to get out of the way.

He caught a glimpse of the object and saw it was a breach-ing ram. Graf wielded it like a baseball bat.

Crane jumped back in time to avoid being battered by a third swing, but in his haste, he didn't watch his footing. As he moved, his right foot skidded on the slick floor, leaving him open. He deflected the blow with his left forearm again, but Graf hit even harder this time. The breaching ram dented the outer plating of his prosthetic, shock jarring through his body.

He threw a punch with his right arm, but Graf dodged, then kicked him back. He tried to slash, but the bionics were damaged. Graf struck again, bending two of the claws out of shape.

Desperate, he leaped backward, allowing himself some breathing space. He knew Graf could only maintain this heightened state for ninety seconds, but assuming he'd attacked directly after triggering the ability, not even a quar-ter of that time had passed. Crane wasn't sure if he could last that long without a change in strategy.

Feigning another arm malfunction, he allowed Graf to land a hit, rolling so the ram glanced off his helmet. Even so, the force was enough to crack his visor. Crane staggered back, and his opponent pressed the advantage.

Moving backward, Crane warded the next blow off with his left, causing further damage to the arm.

The crack in his visor, coupled with the powder residue, reduced his visibility to almost zero. He had to finish the fight now.

Graf laughed.

Crane ignored him, stepping into the nearest room. The enhanced followed, ready to bludgeon him.

As he started over the threshold, Crane touched the screen of his micro-console, dropping all shutters on the level again. A stomach-turning crunch abruptly silenced Graf. His enhancement had no effect on his skeletal structure, which couldn't withstand seventy pounds of reinforced metal slamming down in under a second. The sight was grisly, even for the Mutilator.

Breathing heavily, he paused and took stock. There was no way Graf was getting up again, and the enhanced officer was the last to fall. He'd damaged the bionic arm, and its fingers had completely seized up. Crane could perform a makeshift repair with the maintenance kit, but that would have to wait until he was long gone, before more police came looking.

First things first, he'd have to drag the bodies onto the service elevator so he could take them upstairs and pile them on the roof. That way, the inevitable news helicopters could provide a clear look at his handiwork after he placed an anonymous tip.

Then, he'd have to decide what to do with Sergeant Miller.

It was a shame that he couldn't get his full dozen, but Baxter was right. Eleven out of twelve wasn't bad.

CHAPTER 19

When Miller came to, he had no idea where he was. His neck hurt, his left arm was immobile, and somebody was playing the blues far too loudly.

He was alone in an unfamiliar room. It took a few moments for him to realize where he was, then everything came flooding back—a strike team with the aim to capture the cop killer who'd plagued their department, the building sealing shut and the lights going off, a sharp stinging in the side of his neck, then nothing.

He felt goosebumps rising all over. His hands shook, and he couldn't decide if it was fear or an after-effect of whatever weapon had been used on him. His blaster was gone, as were his radio headset and the buck knife he kept strapped to his ankle. He hadn't brought his UCP handgun, but that would only have been confiscated too.

The Mutilator was thorough. He'd outsmarted them.

Miller was still alive, at least, so that was something. He looked at his arm and saw that it was secured in place by—of all things—a steel manacle bolted to the wall. He wondered who else had been trapped here before him. He wondered if anybody else was still alive. He wondered *why* he was still alive.

Miller was no detective and lacked the insight into the criminal psyche that profilers had. He was a simple beat cop, outraged by the deaths of his fellow officers. His other reason for coming was Vic. They always looked out for each other. So much for that.

The Mutilator could be back at any moment, and the last thing Miller wanted was to be at his mercy. He had to do something.

He examined the shackle. He knew it wouldn't budge, but he tried straining against it anyway. His right hand remained free, but he wasn't within arm's length of anything useful, nor did he have anything in his pockets other than lint, a stick of gum and a token for a half-price coffee at Greasy McGee's. He could've used one.

The door opened, and Miller considered feigning unconsciousness but decided the Mutilator wouldn't be fooled.

He entered, dragging a body behind him. Miller had never seen him in person and honestly, the impression he gave was a little underwhelming.

The Mutilator had removed his helmet, revealing a pale, angular face and a shaven head.

The suit itself was partially covered in some sort of white powder and the notorious claws seemed crumpled. In fact, the entire left arm looked badly damaged, motionless by the killer's side.

Miller could use that to his advantage and felt a glimmer of pride that his team had at least gone down fighting. But judging from his casual approach, the Mutilator had eliminated all immediate threats. That meant Miller was the sole survivor.

"Good evening, Sergeant," the Mutilator said. Miller hadn't expected the smooth British accent. "I must apologize for your current captivity. I can assure you, it wasn't part of my plan."

He knew he shouldn't respond, but he couldn't resist getting in a quip. "You can make it up to me by letting me go."

Seemed like the smartassery of Sergeant Kyle Copeland was rubbing off on him.

The Mutilator chuckled. "I'm afraid I cannot do that. Don't worry, eventually, reinforcements will arrive to free you, though I'll be long gone. In the meantime, I thought you'd want some company."

The body placed in front of him. Even without seeing the face, Miller knew it was Vic. His EDA suit was soaked with blood from four vicious stab wounds along his back. Struck by the urge to be sick, Miller forced himself to look away. Police officers faced the possibility of death every day they put their uniform on, and to come after a cop killer easily doubled that risk.

That knowledge did nothing to lessen the shock of a twenty-five-year friendship ending so abruptly. A gaping hole yawned inside Miller's chest, as it had after Marion.

Somehow, his professional side took over. Pushing aside equal measures of anger, disbelief and shock, he watched the Mutilator leave. He managed to glimpse an ancient service elevator outside, just before the door slid shut and the music stopped.

With his captor gone, Miller knew he had to make a move immediately. He could be next.

Especially now that he'd seen the Mutilator's face.

He looked down at his former partner, hoping for inspiration. Vic's sidearm was still in its holster, but without a live biometric signature, the gun was useless. Rumor had it there were ways to circumvent the safeguards, but they were beyond him.

Seasoned cops often carried a backup weapon, and he knew for a fact his partner did.

Casting his mind back, he tried to recall if Vic had ever told him where it was. He remembered being at a bar while an intoxicated Vic bragged about how "crazy-prepared" he was.

Left foot, thought Miller.

Listening out, he reached over, grabbing hold of his partner's belt, and pulled, dragging his body along the floor until he could reach his foot and remove the boot.

Perpetually sensitive about his height, Vic had always worn two-inch lifts. The enlarged sole provided an ideal hiding place for a small firearm, and Miller prized open the small compartment. Ensconced snugly within was an ultra-compact personal defense blaster.

He removed the gun and examined it. Fractionally smaller than his palm, it bore no sights—electronic or otherwise—and didn't even have a trigger guard. Luckily, as it wasn't approved standard issue, the blaster had no ID system. On the downside, its tiny energy cartridge contained enough power for a single shot, only intended as a last-resort weapon. For him, it certainly was.

He pointed the gun at the door, then decided against it. The blaster wasn't heavy, but he wasn't accustomed to using his right hand and he still couldn't steady it. Besides, assuming he didn't miss altogether, the Mutilator still had his armor on. There'd be repercussions and he'd *still* be trapped. He didn't relish the idea of staring at his dead friend for hours on end until the BMPD finally realized something was wrong and sent back up.

He heard a faint rumbling. The elevator going up. That gave him a little more time.

He looked at his left arm, an idea forming. Risky, certainly, but he was desperate.

Reaching across, he placed the muzzle of the gun to the underside of the manacle. Taking a series of deep breaths to calm his nerves, he looked away, gritted his teeth and squeezed the trigger.

White-hot pain seared through his hand, but he didn't make a sound. Looking again, he saw the bolt had grazed his hand, but more importantly, had sheared through the metal.

He pulled away from the wall, shaking his hand to cool it.

Freeing himself was step one. Now what?

He had to get out of the room.

There was nothing useful in his pockets, and while he didn't hold out much hope Vic's body had anything, he searched anyway.

He turned up a cigarette lighter, and half a packet of coffin nails. Maybe he could start a fire, and somehow overpower the Mutilator when he came to investigate.

He looked around the room. Apart from the mattress, there wasn't a lot of fuel. Very little room either. If the Mutilator didn't come fast enough, Miller would immolate himself.

He needed to start the fire without actually being in the room, which took him back to square one—getting out.

Crouching by the door, he examined it closer.

There. An engraved manufacturer's stamp. *Knox Security Solutions.*

Finally, a stroke of luck. They had doors *everywhere*.

There was a rectangular patch of discoloration on the wall. That must have been where the control panel had been originally. Now it was on the outside, to stop people *leaving*. Miller ran his hand over the patch, recalling having seen the control panels on the outside when the strike team had breached. Had he not been concentrating on the incursion itself, he'd have thought it strange.

Time was running out.

Clenching his jaw, he made a fist with his good hand, then slammed it into the wall.

The plaster cracked but held.

He punched again, and again, then with the fourth blow, the section caved.

Working hurriedly, Miller cleared away the debris, then peered through. He could just make out the back of the control panel.

Using the lighter to see, he opened the access port and went to work on the wires.

Suddenly he stopped and listened.

He could hear the rumbling of the elevator, coming back down.

Not yet, it's too soon!

Nothing for it.

The rumbling stopped.

Footsteps drew nearer and he held his breath.

He'd only get one chance. He'd have to rush the Mutilator, knock him off balance, pin down the working arm…

But the door didn't open and the footsteps passed by.

Miller waited, heart pounding

The seconds dragged by, and then, at last, the elevator started up again.

Miller finally exhaled, then resumed his work.

A minute later, the door slid open.

He poked his head out.

All clear.

He jogged down the hallway to the front door. The door was sealed shut, and there was no control panel to be seen. It must have been installed more recently. Custom job.

He recalled seeing some sort of wrist interface on the Mutilator's arm. That must be what opened the outer doors.

Miller pushed open a door marked "Utility" and looked inside. He found a wrench in an old tool kit; a good makeshift melee weapon. He took a wooden stool, which he used to stand on so he could push a wad of chewed-up gum into the nozzle of the CO2 suppressor on the ceiling.

He waited until he heard the elevator rumbling down, ducked back into the room and used the lighter to set the mattress on fire, then hid around the corner.

"Oh, bugger me!" he heard the Mutilator exclaim, then the sound of running.

Miller rounded the corner in time to see the killer disappear into the burning room.

He hadn't expected that.

Moments later, the Mutilator remerged, coughing from the smoke.

Miller raised the wrench.

The Englishman spotted him.

He swung.

The Mutilator reached up and caught the wrench, pushing it away from him. He only had one arm functioning, but the suit compensated, and it took all Miller's strength to hang on to his weapon. Adrenaline kept him in the fight, but he could feel it wearing off.

He needed an edge.

Glancing down, he spotted the Mutilator's leg holster, a neuro-disruption weapon nestled inside. His neck burned at the memory of it being used on him earlier.

Perfect.

With a surge of energy, he pushed forward, then let go with his right hand and reached for the neuro disruptor. He switched it on, glad it wasn't biometrically operated.

The Mutilator spotted the weapon, and his eyes widened, but it was too late.

Miller pressed the disruptor to the side of his neck.

The killer's body jolted, then went limp.

Miller sighed with relief and released him, letting him slump to the ground. Catching his breath, he crouched down to check for a pulse.

Still alive.

A shameful part of him wanted the Mutilator dead for what he'd done but resolved to let the courts deal with him instead. He'd be more than willing to testify. Maryland had long abolished the death penalty, but God willing, an exception might be made. If so, he would be front row to watch them stick the needle into the son of a bitch's arm.

Satisfied the Mutilator wouldn't be regaining consciousness any time soon, he removed the wrist interface, then used the wrench to pry off pieces of the armor, until only the torso remained. He was surprised to see the left forearm was bionic, but damaged enough not to be a problem.

Pocketing the DigiComm from Vic's body, Miller cuffed the Mutilator, then roughly dragged him out the front door. There, he dropped him unceremoniously and used the DigiComm to call for reinforcements.

Within ten minutes, Sergeant Kyle Copeland and another strike team pulled up, sirens blaring. Miller briefly explained the situation, then watched as the officers cordoned off the street, though it did nothing to deter rubberneckers. News crews would arrive soon.

He promised he'd return to the precinct for a debriefing later; he needed a little time to come to grips with the evening's events. To sweeten the deal, he told Copeland that he could take credit for the capture without having to do any of the paperwork. The young sergeant eagerly accepted.

Miller walked until he found himself at Druid Hill Park. As he sat down on a bench, there was a rumble of thunder and the heavens opened upon him. He didn't care. The weather perfectly mirrored his mood.

PART III

SAVAGE

CHAPTER 20

Baltimore—Present

The tiltrotor touched down at Thurgood Marshall just after two in the morning. Thanks to a call from Collins, Allondra Conway was waiting with a welcoming committee for Crane. Six officers escorted him at gunpoint to a nearby containment van.

"How'd you do?" she asked.

"Alright," said Collins. "Turns out the copycat is Chad Savage."

"The actor guy? No kidding!"

"It's true."

"Did you get him?"

"No. The feds took over, kicked us off the case."

She rolled her eyes. "Typical. Did Crane give you any trouble?"

Collins glanced at Miller, who said nothing. "Nothing we couldn't handle."

"Good to hear. Go home, Collins. Come see me tomorrow to debrief. We'll take his Lordship back to his regular quarters. Miller, you're free to go."

With a nod of dismissal, Conway went to the van and climbed into the passenger seat. Collins went off, probably to find one of the airport's bars, and Miller called for a cab.

On the ride, he rang Donovan, but again, she didn't answer. He texted her a rough outline of the night's events.

He was beyond exhausted by the time he reached home. Gratefully, he staggered up to where the freshly made bed was waiting for him and collapsed onto it. He didn't even have the strength to undress and was asleep moments after his head touched the pillow.

Twelve hours later, he woke, surprisingly refreshed, though his battered body groaned in protest when he moved. A decadently long hot shower took the edge off, and a couple of painkillers helped with the rest. He shot a quick text to Captain Donovan to let her know he wasn't coming in.

Calling for another cab, he fed Spartacus II, grabbed his ID, keys and phone, then headed outside to wait.

In the cab, he thought over the events of the past few days—playing detective, almost overdosing and literally fighting for his life. And now after all of that, they'd been booted from the case, just when they were getting somewhere.

The cab pulled up to Charles Centre One, Miller paid the driver and went in. There was no sign of Allondra Conway, but that didn't bother him. The receptionist opened the visitor's garage for him, and he retrieved his 2050 Phantom.

Driving away, he couldn't shake the feeling he'd be back there all too soon.

Miller spent most of the afternoon wandering around Druid's Park, fresh coffee courtesy of Dopinder in hand. He checked and rechecked his phone, but there were no messages from Donovan or anybody, for that matter. He supposed he should be grateful for the peace.

When he started to get hungry, he decided on a whim to do something he hadn't dared try since Marion had died.

That evening, he managed to reserve a table at Torelli's, after a next-to-last minute cancelation. The little Italian restaurant had been one of their favorites. It felt surreal being there, but despite being alone, Miller actually felt comfortable.

His regular mackintosh and slacks were destined for the dry-cleaners in the morning, so he wore his old sports jacket instead. It was a little tighter than the last time he'd worn it, so he left it unbuttoned and tried not to think about what his wife would say if she could see him in it now.

As he studied the menu, somebody called his name. He looked up to see his sister-in-law across the room.

Miller wasn't sure if he wanted to see Jazz after Friday's incident, but he'd always promised himself to look out for her, for Marion's sake, and motioned her over. She looked tired, but her skin was clearer and she'd regained a little color. Her hair was washed and tied-back for a change, and she wore a modest skirt with a plain top. She seemed unsure what to do with her hands, clearly self-conscious, but not jumpy.

"Hello, Myles," she said, another sign she was in one of her better moods.

"Hello, Jazz."

An uncertain pause, then, "I wanted to talk. Could I sit?"

Miller nodded. "How'd you know I'd be here?"

"Lucky guess."

She hesitated. "I am so sorry about the other day. I'm sorry about breaking my promise about the Stimz and for flipping out on you. Most of all, I'm sorry for taking what happened to Marion out on you. I know you loved her, and that you were doing your best for her."

Miller disagreed with the last part but said nothing.

"After you left, and with Modsy gone, I realized how alone I was, stranded in my enabler's apartment. Again. But it was worse this time because I didn't have you or Marion to help me. And that scared the hell outta me. But then I realized I needed to help myself, so I went down to Charles Street and checked myself in."

Miller didn't reply, busy processing her story. The more he waited, the more nervous she seemed to grow.

"I've been clean forty-eight hours now," she continued. "They let me out under supervision."

She pointed over to where a bored-looking woman stood up against the wall making no effort to be inconspicuous.

"I've got fifteen minutes. If I'm not back in time or I make trouble, I'm out of the program and the police will deal with me instead."

Miller was still looking at her chaperone. Part of him was still mad at Jazz, yet another part wanted to help, regardless. She seemed earnest enough, but talk was cheap. He sighed. Maybe it was the nostalgia of Torelli's, maybe being there made him more connected to Marion, but he decided to meet her halfway.

"You're on thin ice, Jazz, let's be clear about that. But I forgive you."

His sister-in-law looked like she was on the verge of tears. She was about to say something, but he wasn't finished.

"You weren't entirely wrong. I was so concerned with earning enough money to help save Marion that we didn't spend nearly enough time together in her final weeks. I'll always regret that, but at the time, I couldn't let myself give up."

Jazz nodded. "How could you?"

"And I became so focused on working, I also ignored you. So, I'm sorry too."

A faint grin crossed her face. "Thank you, Myles."

He felt as though a huge weight had lifted from his shoulders. He had to admit that it felt good that there was one thing in his life he could do something about.

Making eye contact with the chaperone, he waved her over and showed her his ID. "Sergeant Miller, BMPD. My sister-in-law tells me that you're overseeing her temporary release?"

"Yeah."

"Do you think we can extend her outing a little longer? I'll help supervise and will take full responsibility for her."

The woman looked at him briefly. "Fine. Half an hour."

"I appreciate it."

The woman shrugged, then went to sit at a nearby table.

"Now you can stay for dinner," Miller said.

Jazz beamed.

They ordered and chatted as they waited. Once they'd moved past awkward small talk, their conversation turned to swapping their favorite stories about Marion. Miller soon found he was enjoying himself, and even Jazz looked more relaxed. For five years, he'd tried to talk about his wife as little as possible. Allowing himself to now was cathartic.

After dinner, the chaperone came back to the table to collect Jazz and Miller even felt charitable enough to give her a hug goodbye. He promised he'd try and visit as soon as he could and, depending on her progress, maybe even take her for a day out.

While he'd forgiven her, he hadn't forgotten her actions. She had a long way to go in fully earning back his trust, but as far as first steps went, they'd made good progress that night.

CHAPTER 21

Monday morning was a somber affair, as the BMPD held the memorial service for their fallen officers from the Hippodrome incident. Besides the grieving families, a contingent of officers from several other precincts were also in attendance, including Chief Hesseman.

Though sending his personal condolences, the Commissioner didn't show.

Miller, in full-dress uniform, stood by Captain Donovan as she gave a heartfelt eulogy about each of the officers, managing to keep her composure despite her obvious exhaustion and sorrow at losing some of her best and brightest.

Alvarado, Clarke, Nelson and West took part in a three-volley salute, using ceremonial rifles loaded with blank rounds. Even Wyatt sat in slacks and a blazer.

Lieutenant Copeland was still nowhere to be seen, although Miller had heard Officer Alvarado hadn't stopped looking for him.

Afterward, as the fallen were taken to Green Mount Cemetery to be interred, Wyatt came up to Miller and handed over his cell phone. "Sarge, you're gonna wanna see this."

It was a video. A black screen changed to a countdown, then transitioned to a nondescript room. The angle was too tight to reveal much other than the edge of a bed, and the man who sat on it—Chad Savage, wearing his mechanized suit.

"Wyatt, what am I looking at here?" Miller asked.

"Just watch," the tech said.

Savage spoke, his voice distorted by filters in his helmet.

"Greetings Savages! Today, I'm pleased to announce the event you've all been waiting for. By the weekend, your

Savage King will fight the one and only Metro Mutilator! For my more recent followers, you've probably heard of the individual who terrorized Baltimore's finest boys and girls in blue for three years.

"This aptly-titled Mutilator inspired me to have my own version of the mech suit he made, with a few of my own modifications. Most of you have seen the suit in action before, but that, my loyal fans, was the mere leadup to the ultimate battle, where I will dethrone the original, and prove who the superior warrior is!"

Miller was dumbfounded at the actor's audacity.

"Due to some unexpected interference, however," Savage continued, "there's been a change in plans. But one I guarantee will make things all the more interesting to my loyal Savages."

The actor leaned forward.

"Myles Miller, Ezecki Collins. If you're watching, and I believe this will find you somehow, I am issuing a challenge. A game of sorts between the three of you, a few of my friends and myself. The time and place will be decided shortly and announced later tonight. Given the outcome the last time we played, I understand your reluctance, but consider the prize at stake here. Ask yourselves, 'What would Gregory want?'"

At this, an image of Agent Nichols, bound and blindfolded, flashed onto the screen for several seconds.

"The choice is yours, fellas. But if you don't want my six points to become seven, I'd play ball. As for my loyal Savages, keep watching!"

He gave a thumbs-up, then the video briefly cut to a series of numbers and letters, then ended.

Miller couldn't believe it. "Holy hell."

Half an hour later, Miller sat in Captain Donovan's office with Officers Clarke, Nelson and West.

Dr. Shields and Special Agent Webber joined them from D.C. via satellite link. Wyatt brought them up to speed, and they watched as Webber kicked out at a nearby bench.

"What do we do, Anne?" asked Dr. Shields.

Webber took a deep breath. *"We don't know for sure that's Chad Savage. Anybody could be under there. Whoever it is has kidnapped a federal agent, so this is now a high-priority case.*

"However, until we know more, we keep a lid on this. The more people involved, the more we risk spooking this bastard. If he goes to ground, he'll drag this whole thing out even longer."

"That's the last thing any of us wants," said Donovan.

"Mr. Wyatt, what can you tell me about the video?"

The tech cleared his throat.

"Not a lot; they covered their tracks thoroughly. When a video uploads to OurVid, the file is played through decoding software, which copies all audio and converts it to text format. The transcript is used for closed captioning, but also provides information to agencies like the FBI."

"The feds monitor all our videos?" West asked.

Webber reddened. *"Not exactly. We don't have the time and people power to scour every video on every social network."*

"That's where the flagging system comes in," said Wyatt. "It's an algorithm which automatically sifts through each transcript as it's generated, searching for keywords, such as 'bomb,' or 'militia,' and the names of law enforcement agencies, criminals, missing persons, and certain known insurgent groups. Each occurrence is flagged and the relevant department is notified."

Webber frowned. *"You know an awful lot about it, Mr. Wyatt."*

A note of discomfort crept into the tech's voice. "I helped design the algorithms."

Miller shook his head. He'd always kept social media at arm's length and, having no desire to understand it, this was mostly beyond him.

"Did they set off a flag in our system?" asked Webber.

"I don't think so. He kept his syntax ambiguous in the video. There's not much to attract the attention of your cyber division. But I have my own in place. I picked up a message board out in the dark web referring to the Metro Mutilator. I put out a few digital feelers and found the video. Scuttlebutt says it's the latest in a series."

"There's a bunch of letters and numbers at the end of the video," Miller observed. "What's that about?"

"It's a sequence, correlating to a randomly-generated user-name for an inactive OurVid account. At a pre-determined time established on the message boards, the account activated, revealing an untitled video upload. The video stayed up for half an hour, then it was deleted and the account shut down."

"Then how does he make sure his followers see them?" asked Webber.

"Automatic download probably. Luckily, I managed to copy the original."

"So Crane was right," said Miller. "There's an audience."

"Kung-fu snuff films," said Shields.

"He's killing our people for OurVid views?" asked Webber. *"You can't be serious!"*

"That's the gist of it."

"How many people watch?"

"Couldn't say for sure, but a few hundred stateside at least," said Wyatt. "Who knows how many more outside the country."

"That can't be very lucrative," chimed in Clarke.

"It doesn't have to be," said West. "If it *is* Chad Savage, his legitimate movies make him millions."

"So a side project?" Miller wondered.

"Can you get a fix on his location, Mr. Wyatt?" Agent Webber asked.

"No go, ma'am. I tried pinpointing the origin of the upload and it was from a public identification node; one of those retro internet cafés down in Atlanta, of all places."

Webber rubbed at her chin. *"Alright, we go down and look at the security footage. We'll see who was online there at the time of the upload."*

"Anne," said Dr. Shields. *"I realize I'm just a lowly medical examiner, but should you be chasing that trail? This guy could have you chasing ghosts, and meanwhile, the life of one of our own is in danger."*

"You said so yourself, we can't spook him," Miller added. "If you try to locate him instead of playing ball, he could cut his losses and run."

Webber sagged against the bench. *"You're right. Greg's safety is the number one priority. This asshole has people so scared, the ones bothering to come in are having to pull triple shifts. Guess it's all catching up to me."*

"The BMPD will help out however we can," Donovan said.

"Absolutely," said Miller. "I'll talk to Collins and we'll figure something out. Wyatt, keep an ear to the ground. Let us know about anything regarding Savage."

"Can do."

"And send the video to Conway at Charles Centre. Make sure she and Collins are up to speed. A few of Savage's goons are still in custody. Hopefully, West and I can find out what they know about his plan."

He turned to the junior officer. "If it's alright with you?"

"Anything to help."

Special Agent Webber met Miller and West at Union Station, then took them to the DCMP precinct.

Interrogating the mercenaries was easier said than done.

"What do you mean you let them go?" Miller asked.

The DCMP officer shrugged. "They made bail, so we let 'em go."

"What about the wounded ones?"

The officer typed on their computer. "MedStar Washington Hospital. One's in critical condition."

"Do you know any more than that?"

The officer shook her head.

"Alright, thanks."

———•———

At MedStar, the staff reluctantly let them examine two of the mercenaries. Steve, the one who'd been stabbed, wasn't yet stable and was therefore off-limits.

"The others got off easier," a nurse explained, "but we found traces of Burnout in their system, so we're keeping them sedated in case they lash out and hurt someone."

"That's okay," Miller said.

The nurse left and Officer West put her hand on the head of one mercenary, then the other.

"Well?" asked Miller.

"I'm not getting anything useful. My guess is that Savage is smart enough not to tell them anything until it's time for the next step in his plan."

From the other side of the room, Webber cursed and put her phone away. "I found contact details for Mars Group, but the phone number's been disconnected. Doubt they'll reply to an email either. Any other ideas?"

Nobody came forward with anything.

"Then you'd better get back to Baltimore until your tech guy uncovers something."

"Alright," said Miller.

"Have a safe trip home and notify me the second you come up with anything."

"Will do."

———————•———————

Miller sat with West in a mostly-empty train car, en route to Baltimore. He found this whole situation disquieting. Street gangs and criminal syndicates he could deal with. They almost inhabited a different world entirely.

But these spectators were regular citizens. *What the hell is wrong with the world?* he wondered.

The chime of West's DigiComm broke through his thoughts. Wyatt was calling.

"Savage goofed!" he said proudly. *"He was so preoccupied with being dramatic, he didn't take in his surroundings."*

Wyatt sent a vid through to the DigiComm. It was part of the clip, showing Savage leaning forward, slowed down until it was frame-by-frame.

"Took about two hours to clean up, but this is the end result."

The footage paused. Something was reflected in the visor on his helmet. The subject was distorted, but a long-term Baltimore resident like Miller recognized it straight away. The fifty-one-foot tall aluminum half-man, half-woman statue outside Penn Station. "He's in Baltimore."

"Yup. I pinpointed the hotel from the angle. Donovan sent in a strike team five minutes ago. We still can't find Lieutenant Copeland, so Clarke's leading the team. We even had to put in an urgent request from the neighboring precincts for a few officers to bolster their numbers."

"What? They're just gonna rush in? What if it's a trap?"

"That's what the captain said, but Special Agent Webber started throwing her weight around. She still doesn't think it's actually Savage, but she's keen to nail whoever it is. In fact, she's flying over as we speak."

Miller couldn't believe it. This was the Hippodrome Theatre all over again. Worst of all, he was stuck on a train and helpless do anything about the situation.

Wyatt patched through a live feed from one of the body cams so they could watch.

The breach and subsequent room-clearing were textbook. But nobody was there.

Clarke came into view. *"Chou, get downstairs and talk to the front desk. Apologize for the mess and see if they know anything about Savage and his entourage. If they ask, this was a training exercise."*

The officer nodded and left the room.

"Well, this was a huge waste of time," they heard Officer Nelson complain. They couldn't see him, so presumably his was the body cam they were watching through.

"Maybe not," Clarke said, looking at the cupboard opposite the bed Savage had been sitting on. Inside was a camera mounted on a roving gyro-pod. The little red light on the front indicated it was on and still recording.

"Wyatt, are you getting this?"

"Yup. I'm not picking up any transmission signals. I guess they just left it."

"Maybe he's left a message for us," Miller said.

"Make sure it's safe," Wyatt said, *"then bring it in and we'll take a look."*

CHAPTER 22

Back at the precinct, most of the officers who'd taken part in the strike had been sent home. The others still working the case squeezed into Donovan's office.

Miller saw Special Agent Webber's knuckles whiten as she held her coffee cup. She didn't look like she was coping well.

Somebody knocked at the door.

"Captain Donovan?" It was Lieutenant Heeth from the graveyard shift.

"Yes, Lieutenant?"

"Two guys are here from Orion Security Solutions."

"Who?"

"The company contracted to guard the Hippodrome Theatre while repairs are underway. I can't get ahold of Captain Gouveia."

"Of course," Donovan muttered.

"The guards said they'd been forced out by these real tall guys. Military types with grey eyes."

Mars Group.

"Are the guards still out there?" Donovan asked.

"Only the two that didn't wind up in the ER. They keep asking who's gonna reimburse them for their broken DigiComms."

"Thank you, Lieutenant. I'll look into it in a moment."

"I guess we've found them," Miller said.

Wyatt came in, digital pad in hand. "Captain, I've got it!"

Connecting wirelessly to Donovan's computer, he played the vid on over the holographic display for them all to see.

Savage was in the hotel room, still wearing his suit.

"Hello, Savages. Once again, I gotta move up my production schedule. Myles, Phineas, and Ezecki, evidently you saw my last video, so hopefully, you're watching again. Thanks to you, the big showdown is happening even earlier than planned. Turn up to the Hippodrome Theatre tomorrow without your firearms or electronics of any kind. You'll have to rely on your wits and your fists. A knife or a nightstick, if you're clever about it. Don't worry, my guys will be the same. We wanna keep this interesting, after all."

Miller noticed Savage conveniently neglected to mention their other advantages—his enhancement and their use of Burnout.

"How you choose to fight is up to you, but be assured, we will be fighting to kill. And I know what you're thinking. What's stopping us from storming the place with a strike team or two? Well, allow me to introduce my little deterrent."

The actor produced his phone and displayed a set of blueprints.

Wyatt paused the footage.

"What are we looking at here?" asked Webber.

"Big Boy II," he said. "You know how the military donated one of their ionic particle cannons to us?"

"How could I forget?" Donovan asked wryly.

"Savage must have the other one."

"And that's a problem?" asked Webber.

"Very much so," said Wyatt, unpausing the video.

"Your tech boys probably recognize this little baby and what happens if we juice it up."

Wyatt paused the video again. "*That's* the problem. In battle, IPCs had a failsafe function in case the encampment was ever overrun. As a last-ditch effort to prevent equipment from falling into enemy hands, the operator could remotely trigger a core overload and blow the whole thing."

"Sounds drastic," said Captain Donovan. "And expensive."

"That's why the military discontinued them," Wyatt said.

"Why would *we* use something like that?" Miller asked.

"Lieutenant Copeland's the only one who ever tried," said Wyatt. "And only after I disabled the overload failsafe. I guess Savage isn't showing the same consideration."

Wyatt resumed the video.

"If anybody else decides to gatecrash, let's just say we'll have a heck of a party favor that'll really blow you away!" continued Savage, chuckling at his own joke. "I wouldn't get trigger happy either. You won't know who, but three of my guys are packing dead man switches. If you don't want festivities kicking into overdrive prematurely, I suggest looking before you leap.

"This is an exclusive party. Anybody turns up who isn't Phin, Myles or Ezecki, we'll shut the whole thing down. And if anybody else tries to leave early, we'll get upset. That goes for the rest of the block too. Filming begins at one o'clock sharp, so don't be late. See you then, boys, and remember to play nice.

"To the rest of my Savages, keep watching!"

Savage held up the phone again, displaying the sequence of numbers and letters, and the video ended.

Agent Webber broke the silence. "Mr. Wyatt, what happens if that cannon detonates?"

"There'll be a wave of pure ionic energy," the tech replied. "Anything within a four-hundred-yard radius will be obliterated."

Miller felt a chill down his spine. Of all the places for that to happen, the heavily populated Central Baltimore was one of the worst.

"He can't be serious," said Captain Donovan. "They'll be killed too!"

"But he'll go down in infamy," said Miller. "I think that's his end-game. And Mars Group don't have long life expectancies, so they won't care."

"It's gotta be a bluff."

"Can you afford to take the chance, Captain?" Agent Webber asked.

Miller knew they couldn't. Not only were hundreds of civilian lives now at stake, but the infrastructural damage would also be immense. Furthermore, the public would demand to know why the BMPD hadn't prevented such a tragedy. No amount of funding or PR spin could counteract that. They could be out of a job by the end of the week.

On the other hand, if they succeeded, it might just prove they were worth keeping around. As far as Miller was concerned, they didn't have a choice. And knowing Donovan, the captain thought the same way.

Donovan turned to Wyatt. "Get the word out. Send for every available officer from the Central, South, Southeast and Eastern Precincts, priority one. Cordon off the entire neighborhood and evacuate as many people as we can from the surrounding area."

"What about the people inside?" Miller asked.

"We'll have to put them into lockdown."

"Shouldn't we be getting the civilians *away* from the blast zone?"

"Yes, but Savage said he'll detonate the device if anyone leaves."

His left hand curled into a fist. "People could die, Fiona!"

"You think I don't know that?" Donovan didn't even raise her voice. "Right now, we are on the backfoot. The only thing we can do is try to minimize casualties as best we can."

"There shouldn't be *any* casualties."

"Then you'd better make damn sure you beat that son of a bitch and disable the IPC, Myles."

Miller knew from her tone of voice that this wasn't an argument he could win. Donovan would fire him first. But he knew she was also right.

"Don't get me wrong," she continued. "Those deaths will be on us all. We just have to do what they want until we can find an opening to strike."

"Fine."

"Wyatt, we need people calling each residence and warning them to stay inside until this is over. Call it a drill, a gas leak, whatever. Work in shifts if that's what it takes.

"Got it," said Wyatt.

"Is that alright with you, Agent Webber?"

"Sound solid," the fed replied. "I'll liaise with the local media outlets and find a way to get the message out without causing too much panic. We can't keep everything from the public, but hopefully, we can minimize the fallout."

She turned to Miller. "Put me in touch with whoever is supervising Phineas Crane. He and Mr. Collins will need to be kept appraised of the situation."

"We're really going to let him out again?" asked Miller.

"He didn't try anything last time," said Webber. "Apparently he has some sort of fascination with you, so it's a good thing you're you're going too." The agent left to make some calls.

Miller couldn't believe what he was hearing, but as he didn't feel like spending time in a federal penitentiary, he said nothing.

"Myles," said Captain Donovan, "go home."

"You're kidding! I need to stay and help."

"There are innocent lives at stake here, so no, I'm not," Donovan said, before softening. "I know it's hard to be sidelined, but there isn't anything more you can do tonight. Regroup here tomorrow at midday when it's your turn at bat, but until then, get some rest. You're in for the fight of your life.

"Dismissed, Sergeant."

Sensing an argument he couldn't win, Miller agreed. After sending Webber the contact details for Allondra Conway, he bid them goodnight and caught a cab home.

CHAPTER 23

Though still feeling tired the next day, Miller had slept better than he thought he would. At ten-thirty, he showered, changed clothes and readied himself as best he could.

He picked up his mackintosh from the dry cleaners. Pulling the coat on over his EDA vest was a strangely comforting sensation, and when he completed the ensemble by slapping on his battered homburg, he felt more like himself.

He took an old cardboard box from his storage cupboard. Inside was a handful of spare bullets for his UCP handgun. He cleaned the gun, just as his father had shown him, and then loaded a handful of bullets into the box magazine.

Feeling as ready as he could be, he headed to Charles Centre One for what he hoped, but doubted, would be the last time. Conway met him, joking about setting up a cot for him in one of the cells. He attempted to laugh politely, but he was more focused on the challenge ahead.

"I'm starting the countdown again," Conway said. "If I don't hear from you or Ezecki, I'll have to assume the worst and take executive action."

Miller wondered what the hell she meant, then remembered the micro-capsules Collins had mentioned. He hadn't fully believed Collins, but this confirmed he'd been telling the truth. He made a mental note to investigate further, provided he survived the next few hours.

In the deepest sublevel of the facility, Phineas Crane was once again being released from his holding cell. Under the watchful eyes of Collins and Conway, he was refitted with the plastic prosthesis, manacled, then escorted across the gangway.

Crane said nothing, simply tilting his head down in a slight nod toward Miller.

The elevator ride back up passed in silence. As they exited, the doors closed behind with what Miller felt was a certain finality.

"How much have you been told?" he asked Crane.

"As much as I assume I'm allowed to know," he replied. "I'm aware of the challenge and I am aware of the stakes."

"You were right. We hadn't seen the last of Savage."

"Egocentric oik," Crane muttered. "Still, it's nice to get out of that bloody cell again. I rather feel like a heavyweight champion, returning to defend his hard-won title."

"Shut up, Crane," said Conway, nudging him in the back with her pulse rifle.

●——————————●

As their van reached Park Avenue, two squad cars and another van were leaving. Wyatt, Officer Nelson and Special Agent Webber were the only ones to be seen.

"Where's everybody going?" Miller asked.

"We're leaving now," Agent Webber said. She pointed over to where one of the Mars Group mercs was standing in the middle of the road. His name tag read "Bob." Miller recognized him as one of the ones he'd stunned at the penthouse back in DC.

Spotting them, the mercenary waved back, displaying a small cylindrical object. His thumb depressed an orange button on the side. Miller knew that if Bob released the button even momentarily, the particle cannon would overload, meaning they couldn't shoot him.

"This joker came over twenty minutes ago, waving a white handkerchief," Webber said. "Told us if they see any uniform in sight from here to North Greene Street by one o'clock, they'll detonate. From here on out, you're on your own."

"Alright," said Miller.

Crane looked at the special agent thoughtfully. "You have something else up your sleeve, don't you?"

Webber hesitated. "Just focus on the fight, Crane. Let us worry about the rest."

"Well, how about it, Crane?" Miller asked. "Are you going to give us trouble?"

"Certainly not," he said. "I intend to see this through to the bitter end. It's a matter of honor."

"And what about afterward?"

"As much as I've enjoyed my freedom, I have no desire to antagonize you, Sergeant. Once matters are settled, I'll submit myself back into your custody."

"I'll hold you to that. Don't make me regret this."

Conway seemed satisfied when Crane agreed but kept her pulse rifle trained on him anyway.

"Well, then, let's not keep the nice psychopath waiting," Crane said.

Webber signaled to the mercenary, who walked over, keeping a distance of several yards between them.

Bob fished a phone out of his pocket and pointed it at Crane. "Wave to the camera, boys!"

Crane, Collins and Miller did so. Presumably, he was showing his boss that all three men had shown up.

Miller handed his blaster over to Wyatt.

"Good luck, Sarge."

"Thanks, Wyatt."

"That goes double for me," said Webber. "We're all counting on you."

"No pressure then," Miller said wryly.

Collins dumped his gun into the trunk of Webber's hired car. "Let's get this over with."

Nelson, Webber and the civilians climbed into the car and drove to a makeshift command center a few blocks away.

"Alright, boys," said Mercenary Bob. "Stay ten feet behind me at all times 'til I say so. Unless you wanna kick things off early."

"As you wish," replied Crane.

The three men waited for Bob to get ahead, then followed him down West Fayette Street.

"Any advice?" Miller asked Crane.

"Fight to win. The longer the fight, the more likely you are to lose, especially with the Burnout in their systems."

"Savage handed you your ass on a silver platter last time," said Collins. "What makes you think this will be any different?"

Crane paused and looked at Bob. The mercenary gave no indication of being able to hear them, but the Mutilator lowered his voice all the same.

"I underestimated him last time. But now, I have his measure. I can get inside his head."

Bob paused at the doorway of the theatre. With an exaggerated bow, he gestured for them to enter.

Miller cast a final glance up at where the BMPD had blasted a hole through the second floor. That damage had come from a short, concentrated burst. He shuddered to think what kind of destruction a full-on detonation would wreak.

He shook himself, re-focused and followed the others into the Hippodrome.

CHAPTER 24

B ob waited for them inside.

"Through there." He pointed to the electronics scanner.

Crane passed through first. Examining the image on the monitor, Bob gave the all-clear and reset the scanner.

Miller went next, placing his phone, ID and watch into the InstaPlas tray, and walked through.

Looking up, he noticed one of the cameras from the hotel set in front of the box office, another at the foot of the nearby staircase. He wondered how many had been set up throughout the theatre, and what other surprises might be waiting.

The Mars Group mercs had clearly been busy setting up equipment and familiarizing themselves with the layout of the building. The Burnout would have allowed them to work throughout the night, keeping them awake and alert far more efficiently than most forms of caffeine could and negating a need for shifts.

"Alright, listen up," called Bob, motioning with his detonator. "At one o'clock, the cameras start rolling and your fight begins. Don't start before then; we have a guy monitoring the feeds.

"Collins, you're going to the left; your opponent will be waiting for you in the bar near the side entrance. Miller, you're going upstairs to what's left of the café. Mr. Crane, as the main attraction, you're right through here."

Striding over to the polished oak-paneled doors to the theatre proper, he flung them open. "Better get moving."

Miller watched the others go, then walked up the stairs. With some effort, he managed to banish his former memories of the place, both the bittersweet ones with Marion and the horrible ones from the previous week. He needed to focus on the present.

Reaching the café, he saw his opponent. His nametag read "Grant" and he stood behind a line of yellow electrical tape. Miller spotted a second line about five feet before it, which he assumed was his own mark. Three cameras mounted on roving gyropods with motion tracking were set up around the space and a digital clock sat on top of the counter.

Seven minutes to go.

"So, you're the guy who took down the Mutilator," Grant said. "You're older than I thought."

Miller said nothing in reply. He stood where he was supposed to stand, running through the possible ways their fight could pan out. The mercenary shrugged off his jacket and slowly turned on the spot, revealing the absence of any gun or another weapon.

The younger man made a few more attempts to rile him up, but Miller was in the zone.

———•———

Downstairs, Collins found himself facing Adam, the de facto leader of Mars Group. Like Bob, he held one of the detonators. Ever since Collins had first laid eyes on him at the Butler Parkes Centre, he'd wanted to punch him right in his stupid lantern jaw.

"I know you from somewhere, don't I?" asked Adam. "Before the party."

"Tried out for Mars Group a few years back," Collins said.

"I remember now! You didn't make the grade."

"I passed the physical and psych evaluations."

"But you were too old to run with us."

Collins snorted. "I can still handle you, junior."

Adam considered him with amusement. "What say we make this interesting then?" He twisted the lower part of the detonator. "Now when I release the switch, there'll be a sixty-second delay. Then, either you take me out, I put you down or we all blow sky high."

Collins looked at the mercenary, incredulous. "You can't be serious?"

"What's wrong, old-timer? Adam taunted. "Worried you aren't fast enough?"

"Not at all. Just wondering what I'll do with my remaining fifty-five seconds."

"That's more like it." Adam grinned.

Collins knew the macho bragging and posturing didn't serve much of a purpose, but it got him in a mindset to fight.

Fight and win.

———————•———————

Crane ignored the doors slamming shut behind him, maintaining his focus on his surroundings instead. He'd never been to the Hippodrome before, which was a shame, as he liked the look of it. It was no Royal Albert, but it had a certain charm to it.

Pity about the other occupant.

"I knew you couldn't resist my invitation!" Savage called from the lit stage.

"Hard to ignore a bomb threat."

"Before that, I mean. Got you out of your cell, didn't I?"

A fair point.

Savage was fully armored but for his helmet, with several mounted cameras and a digital timer set up on a stand and a large cylindrical object covered by a big black sheet. It was about the size of one of the old telephone booths, and Crane had a sneaking suspicion as to what it was. He counted another half-dozen cameras spread throughout the hall, ready to film the action from all angles.

"My, haven't we been busy?" he said, approaching the stage.

"I hoped you would appreciate it," said Savage. "Especially considering the short turnaround time. We had to pull an all-nighter but it's up and running now. Welcome to the show, Phineas Crane. It's great to meet you properly. I'm a huge fan!"

"The pleasure's all yours," Crane replied dryly. "You'll have to forgive me if I don't shake your hand."

"Of course," said Savage. "By the way, I wanted to make things more interesting, so I took the liberty of getting you a little present."

With a flourish, Savage whipped away the cloth. Underneath was a mechanical frame Crane was very familiar with. In the middle of the frame, was his old Wraith suit.

He felt a shiver run down his spine.

Somehow, Chad Savage had not only gotten ahold of the suit, including the cybernetic left arm, but also the housing rack Crane used to put the suit on himself. Judging by the blinking lights on the control panel, the rack had fresh power cells inserted.

The last time he'd seen of the suit, it had been brought in as evidence in his trial. If Savage had been able to appropriate it from the lockup, he was potentially smarter and more well-connected than Crane had initially given him credit for.

Mostly, he felt a thrill at seeing the suit again.

"Do you like it?" Savage asked.

"How the bloody hell did *you* get it?"

Savage smirked. "Guy's gotta have *some* secrets, Phinny. But let's just say the BMPD's security ain't what it used to be. I doubt they even know it's missing."

Crane hoisted himself up onto the stage.

He was drawn to the suit, but instinct told him not to get too close. Savage backed away, giving him space.

"Go on, Phin. Suit up."

Crane circled the housing rack, searching for anything out of place. Everything seemed in order. Gingerly, he stepped up onto the footplate and spread his arms against the frame.

"You know, my agent is angling for me to branch out into theatre," Savage said, casually. "I wouldn't mind coming back here."

"Oh yes? Somehow, I can't picture you tackling the works of Marlowe."

"I think he meant something more autobiographical."

"Naturally. Your favorite subject *would* be yourself."

"Ouch." Savage feigned a hurt expression. "Harsh, but fair."

"Don't worry, Chad, I promise to give you and your audience a better fight this time."

"Even though you've been declawed?"

"Yes. I'll be damned if I let some actor beat me again."

Piece by piece, the armor enclosed around Crane. Torso first, feet, legs and arms.

"You can't stop progress, Phin."

"Progress?" Crane snorted. "You're nothing but a pale imitation."

"Now, now, Phinny," chided Savage. "Is that any way to treat your fans?"

"What do I care about your viewers?"

"I'm talking about me!"

Crane closed his eyes with an exasperated sigh. "Most admirers settle for an autograph, not a fight to the death."

"Guess I just like to go above and beyond."

The Wraith suit self-activated and disengaged from the rack. Crane tested the suit's articulation. Everything seemed to be in working order. "I suppose I ought to be flattered by all this, but you're perverting my mission and I cannot allow you to continue."

"What mission?" asked Savage. "You killed cops, I kill federal agents. Other than being more ambitious, what's the difference?"

"The difference is that I fight for what I believe in. I only went after the crooked and the corrupt. *I* was killing in the name of justice. *You* just want more attention. And now you've got it."

"How noble," Savage sneered. "But you're wrong, Phinny. I'm fighting for what I believe in too."

Crane scoffed. "And what would that be?"

"I believe in myself," Savage said. "I believe in my legacy. Does that make me a narcissist? Sure. But people will remember me like they'll remember you."

"You think the FBI would allow a blight like you on their image? I can guarantee they're covering up your little exploits."

"That won't matter soon," Savage said, gesturing to the closest camera. "My Savages see everything, and when the time is right, they'll share my legacy with the world."

"And the world will revile you."

Savage shrugged. "Good. I'd rather be hated than ignored. At least I'll stand out."

"You'll need to," Crane retorted. "Sun-kissed Adonises like you are a dime a dozen."

Savage clapped his hands and pointed to Crane. "Exactly. So I expand myself. I'll direct or join the UFC. Hell, I could go into politics. The sky's the limit for me. And if they still won't remember me, I'll show them how I killed those agents and how I'm gonna kill you. I wanna be more than famous. I wanna be infamous."

"Is that your Apollo acceptance speech?"

Savage grinned. "Could be."

"What a shame it'll have to be read posthumously," Crane said. "I'm no oracle, but I can tell you this—you will not survive today."

To Crane's surprise, Savage remained nonchalant. "Then so be it." He donned his helmet. "At least I've tried doing something with my life."

Crane considered the actor before him. This went beyond mere bravado. Chad Savage showed no fear. He was ready to seize victory or accept death. It was just another way to challenge himself. In some perverse way, Crane almost respected him for it. But his actions were still an unforgivable affront.

Even though some of the denting had been repaired on his suit, Savage's armor was in much better shape. He'd remounted the cutting laser and, unlike Crane's, his armor still had offensive capabilities in the form of its tapered claws.

Crane had to admit, their design looked sturdier than his own detachable set and probably didn't damage as easily. On the other hand, he had far more experience using his suit. It was an extension of himself and he intended to fully exploit that.

The combatants faced each other behind their respective lines. Their suits contrasted as much as their wearers. Savage's was shiny, black with the flame decals as showy as his fighting style; Crane in his somewhat battered, practical gray and navy armor.

"Welcome to the show, my Savages!" announced Savage. In his peripherals, Crane saw the recording lights of the cameras, realizing they were now live. "As promised, your Savage King is here with Baltimore's very own Metro Mutilator. It's old versus new in a rumble for the ages. Any words for the people at home, Phinny?"

"This is your show, Chad, so I'll keep it short," said Crane, putting on his own helmet. "Good luck, and may the best man win."

"We'll see," Savage said, "as we enter the final countdown."

Savage shifted to a low stance, while Crane kept still. The timer beeped as it reached the last five seconds. There was a sustained chime.

Savage surged forward and Crane ran to meet him. Savage telegraphed a high jumping kick.

Predictable, thought Crane, as he rolled under the attack. Landing close to the edge of the stage, Savage went into a spinning heel kick, but he had moved well out of the way. The actor gave chase, letting loose a series of snapping kicks Crane easily avoided.

You're testing me, Crane thought. *Putting on a show.*

This time, as Savage moved in, Crane twisted aside and kicked out, connecting with a knee joint. Savage responded by slashing out with his claws, barely missing his head. Moving like lightning, Crane seized his arm, yanking Savage off balance and executing a leg sweep.

As Savage broke his fall with a stuntman's ease, then pushed up with his arms and kicked out. Crane couldn't move fast enough to avoid it but managed to bring his arms up in time to take the brunt of the kick, which packed enough of a wallop to lift him a few inches back off the floor. Landing, he bent at the knees, then sprang several feet backward, out of range.

He looked at his bionic arm, which had sustained a few more dents but was still operational.

Savage was back on his feet in a flash. Instead of charging again, he leveled the mounted laser at him and fired. Crane already had his right arm up, plating absorbing the beam and dispersing the energy across its surface.

The cutting laser had a higher, more sustained energy output than a blaster, however, and would start melting through the armor unless he did something. Keeping his arm out in front of him, he closed the distance. Ordinarily, he'd maneuver around Savage and cut the power feed, but without his claws, he'd have to try something else.

A mere yard from Savage, he zig-zagged, shifting from foot to foot. As the actor tried to move the beam quickly enough to keep him pinned, Crane launched himself forward with his right foot and brought his fist smashing down on the emitter.

The device crumpled and sparked, forcing Savage down on one knee. Cursing, he slashed upward, his claws puncturing the side of Crane's suit. Fortunately, the claws didn't go deep enough to hit his body, and he responded by driving his elbow into the side of his opponent's head, denting the helmet and cracking the visor.

Rising, Savage yanked his hand free and kneed him in the chest, though his awkward angle dulled the force and Crane did little more than rock backward. Pressing the advantage, he unleashed a fierce combination of punches, but again, Savage was too fast and he hit empty air each time. Savage feinted left, then brought his leg around in an ax kick, hitting him in the shoulder. He rolled with the impact.

Using the momentum, he spun, balling his fists together and hammering them into Savage, cracking his visor again.

Snarling a string of curses, the actor fired back with a barrage of blows. Many went wild, and Crane managed to deflect one or two until the claws stuck home again, slashing across the right arm of his suit. The monomolecular bonded edges nicked him, drawing blood. It wasn't a deep cut, but the claws had severed most of the circuitry and even part of the titanium framing.

Raising his right leg, he kicked out, pushing Savage away, who went into a roll to gain distance.

With a few moments of reprieve, Crane set about hastily detaching the now-immobile right arm of his suit. Though it left part of him more exposed, he needed the dexterity.

Across the stage, Savage ripped off the remnants of his mounted laser and removed his helmet. The actor charged again, but at the last second, dodged aside and took a flying leap off the edge of the stage. His foot landed on a seat in the front row. It buckled beneath the weight, but he was already jumping to the next row.

Oh no you bloody don't!

Crane launched himself after him.

CHAPTER 25

Upstairs, Miller faced off against Grant. The moment the timer reached zero, the mercenary snatched up a stanchion near the counter, unhooking the velvet rope. He swung, but Miller moved back and the fixture missed him by a hair's breadth. Grant overbalanced and he stepped in and tagged him with a right cross.

Grant brought the stanchion around again and Miller ducked, then charged, plowing a shoulder into him. The pair slammed into the counter and the makeshift weapon clattered to the ground. Grant reached over and grabbed the clock, crashing it down onto his back, causing him to let go.

Shoving him back, Grant swung a wild punch. Miller brought up his arm, deflecting the hit and responding with a body blow. Grant tried for an elbow strike and again he blocked. Miller knew the younger man could outlast him, but he could see he was getting aggravated by his methodical fighting. Any moment, he'd start fighting dirty, like any good mercenary.

Grant aimed a kick at his knee. Of course it would have been the wounded one.

Miller roared in agony and collapsed to his knees. He felt Grant grab the back of his coat, probably intending to haul him up and smash his head open on the bar. But his fall had just been a gambit, giving him the opportunity to grab the Buck 110 Folding Knife from his leg sheath. Shaking off the feeling of déjà vu, he flicked it open and plunged the blade into the mercenary's knee.

Clearly stunned by the sight, Grant didn't make a sound. Miller grabbed the handle and twisted. Apparently, the pain was enough to break through the haze of Burnout, tearing a scream from the man that cut short when the sergeant punched him square in the throat.

Miller watched as he dropped to the ground, choking and spluttering. His knee ached, but he could ignore it for the time being.

He limped over to where the stanchion lay and picked it up. The mercenary looked shocked. Probably not just because of the sudden, brutal attack, but that a man nearly twice his age had gotten the better of him.

Miller stepped around him and swung the stanchion, cracking it against Grant's skull.

He crouched beside the mercenary, feeling for a pulse. It was faint, but there. He rolled him into the recovery position and tied his hands using the man's own belt. If he was concussed or worse, it was his own damn fault. Once he went for a weapon, all bets were off.

Holding down the leg with his knee, he extracted his buck knife, wiped off the blood and slid it back into its sheath. Mercenaries weren't the only ones who could fight dirty.

Ignoring the cameras, he searched Grant's pockets, finding only a miraculously intact DigiComm. He slipped in the earpiece, hoping he might be able to pick up any enemy chatter. The stanchion made for a good improvised weapon, so he grabbed that too. It wouldn't do much against a blaster, but it was better than nothing.

Cautiously, he advanced down the stairs. He hoped he'd be able to help one of the others or even find Agent Nichols.

At the bar, Collins was taking a beating, his head snapping aside with a right hook. He could tell Adam was pulling his punches, savoring the time until he had to press the switch on the detonator again. Which is exactly what Collins wanted.

He kept his guard up, lowering only to try for a swing and allowing Adam to land a hit here and there. He didn't see what was in Collins' hand until it was too late. Adam's right connected below the ribs and Collins clamped something around his wrist which snapped shut with a click.

The man looked down in dull surprise. Collins had fastened one bracelet of a handcuffs around his wrist. With no electronic components, they'd gone undetected by the scanner. The other cuff was attached to Collin's left wrist.

Adam tried lashing out, but the sergeant controlled his right arm and pulled him off balance when he tried to bring around his free arm. Collins had no such restrictions and took the opportunity to batter the mercenary until he dropped the detonator. He kicked Adam behind the knees, who collapsed.

His hand dived into his jacket and brought out an auto-injector. Ripping off the safety cap with his teeth, he plunged the needle into Adam's neck. The mercenary rose, throwing his weight into Collins, who braced himself, then dealt a glancing blow to the side of his head.

Collins bent and scooped up the detonator, holding the switch down.

"The hell… you do…" Adam gasped, unsteady on his feet.

"Just a little epinephrine," Collins said innocently. Pocketing the detonator, he shoved Adam over and pinned him against the top of the bar. The extra adrenaline reacted with the meta-monocluptose already in the merc's system, causing his heart to beat faster and faster, just as Miller's had done.

In the throes of tachycardia, Adam thrashed feebly, but Collins held him firm, counting down the seconds in his head. At thirty, he quickly pressed the switch again, resetting the timer. He felt the merc's pulse plummet as his heart gave out and his ragged breathing stopped. Adam twitched a few more times, then was still.

Collins fished the handcuff key from his pocket and released himself, affixing the shackle to Adam's other arm and flinging his body to the ground. His feeling of satisfaction at outwitting his opponent was compounded by knowing any accusations of excessive force could be justified.

Unconcerned, he kicked over the cameras, busted the lock on the bar fridge and helped himself to a refreshing bottle of Dixon's Dry. Who was to say one of the mercenaries hadn't taken it?

———————•———————

Outside, Officer West stood watching the mercenary standing by the loading bay as he lit up another cigarette. She'd performed a remote facial scan with her DigiComm and ran it against the BMPD database.

Nicholas Folger was ex-military and had a prior for drunk and disorderly about five years before. Other than that, the file was empty.

West had to find a way to incapacitate him without raising any alarms or starting a firefight with a former Green Beret.

She was wearing dark glasses, carrying a handbag and a white cane, and she hoped the disguise would work. "Excuse me?"

The merc turned, hand flying to his jacket. He looked confused.

"Is someone there? I can smell cigarette smoke."

The merc relaxed. "Yeah, I'm here."

"Could you help me out? My boyfriend was supposed to pick me up an hour ago and my cell phone is dead."

Folger frowned. "You shouldn't be here, lady. Turn around and go back."

"Where is everyone?" West asked, doing her best to sound bewildered.

"You need to leave."

"I will. But could I borrow your phone, just to call him real quick?"

Folger sighed. As she reached out to take the phone, his eyes glanced down, spotting the bulge of her DigiComm under the sleeve of her turtleneck. She reached toward his face, but he grabbed her wrist and twisted. Gasping, West cursed herself for being too slow.

Before she could fight back, Folger grabbed the front of her sweater and tossed her over his hip to the ground. He knelt on her abdomen, pulled his sidearm and pointed it at her. "Who the hell are you?"

With one arm trapped beneath her body and the other pinned by Nick, West couldn't use her enhancement. She was helpless.

"You're a cop, aren't you?"

West said nothing.

"You shouldn't have done that. Now we're gonna have to blow the joint."

"Do it," choked West.

He chuckled. "That's the spirit."

But West hadn't been talking to him. On a rooftop three blocks away, she knew Officer Clarke was lying in wait, watching everything through the scope of a TriCore 500 Longshot Rifle. She knew he wouldn't risk shooting until he was sure the mercenary didn't have a detonator and she'd just confirmed it.

The man's head snapped back and he was dead before he hit the ground.

"Thanks," said West.

She picked up Folger's DigiComm, looked at the channel it was set to and adjusted hers accordingly. Flicking back to her pre-set, she spoke to Clarke. "How are we looking?"

"All clear," he reported, *"as far as I can see."*

"Alright, keep an eye out," she said. "I'm going in."

"Be careful, Immi."

"I will."

Switching back to the other channel, she listened intently. Picking up nothing, she drew her sidearm, counted to three in her head and advanced into the loading bay. There were a few pallets and crates, nothing out of the ordinary. Then she saw a jeep parked adjacent to the ramp and ducked behind a forklift when she spotted a mercenary sitting in the driver's seat.

She waited, holding her breath and hoping she hadn't been spotted. When nothing happened, she risked another peek. The mercenary was looking at something and she wondered if it was the IPC.

Lowering herself to the concrete floor, she began a commando crawl toward the vehicle. She wished she wasn't in her civvies as her uniform afforded more protective padding. Nevertheless, she persisted, and soon she was crouched by the jeep, wondering what her next move should be.

Her earpiece crackled to life. *"Nick, what's the situation?"*

There was an odd echo effect as she heard the man both over the DigiComm and in person a few feet away.

"Nick, buddy?"

West heard the door open and braced herself. The merc climbed out, blaster in one hand and what she assumed was one of the detonators in the other.

Quietly placing her own sidearm on the floor, she stood and, after a brief hesitation, lunged toward him. She clamped her hand down on the detonator, while simultaneously placing her other hand against the side of his head, focusing on channeling her enhancement.

The mercenary went rigid, then began to slump. Breathing heavily from the strain, West shifted her body so that she braced him up against the jeep. Keeping the switch on the detonator depressed, she eased it out of his grip.

Letting him drop, she took a roll of electrical tape from the handbag and wrapped a length around the detonator to keep the switch down. After catching her breath and reorienting herself, she used the rest of the roll to bind the merc. It wasn't the best solution, but her enhanced attack would keep him out for at least ten more minutes, and she could always hit him again.

Retrieving her blaster, she took aim as she slowly opened the back door of the jeep.

Inside, was a large object concealed by a tarpaulin. Gingerly, she pulled the tarp aside.

The cannon hummed ominously and an LCD screen blinked at her as she put in a call through her DigiComm. "Wyatt? West. I found it."

"*Is it active?*"

"I'm gonna go with yes. I don't see any power cables."

"*They must be using supercells,*" Wyatt said. "*One of those puppies can keep the cannon running for twenty-four hours or one hundred, five-second bursts, plus an ancillary cell to overload it if necessary.*"

"Good to know," she replied curtly.

"*You remove the supercells, nobody blows up.*"

This proved easier said than done. The only way to access the cells was to open a hatch via the touchscreen, which was locked. The IPC predated biometrics ID but still required a code. West used her enhancement to scan the merc's mind, but he didn't know the code, only Savage did.

Wyatt began compiling a list of likely options. Just as she was about to start keying in the first option, a thought occurred to her. "Wyatt, I need you to look up a specific date for me."

"What do you need?"

CHAPTER 26

Crane chased Savage across the rows of chairs.

Every now and then, Savage doubled back, trying to land a kick, but Crane kept moving out of the way.

Deep down, he was almost enjoying the challenge but decided it was time to take charge. Stopping, he stood with each foot in a seat, trying not to think of them giving way. "Diverting as this is, shouldn't we get back to the fight?"

Savage ignored him, evidently preoccupied with performing for his viewers. Crane moved to the nearest camera and knocked it over. The act felt petty, but it did the trick. Furious, Savage raced over the chairs toward him, and Crane led them back to the stage. Risking a look at his suit's power level, he saw it had dropped to seventy-three percent.

So, that's your game, thought Crane. *But you're getting reckless, my friend. Any moment now, you'll slip up.*

Sure enough, as Savage reached the stage, his foot slipped. As he struggled to maintain balance, Crane moved in to attack. At the last second, however, the actor threw himself forward, somersaulting past him and onto surer ground.

Damn it, thought Crane. *But you'll foul up again.*

Before either fighter could make another move, the theatre went dark. It seemed the BMPD had managed to get the power off. He switched on the night vision function in his visor and looked at Savage. Without his helmet, the actor was disoriented in the near-total blackness.

Quietly, Crane circled around, looking for the best place to strike. He wanted to finish the fight swiftly.

Miller wouldn't approve, but he believed that Savage had to die today. Not just as a matter of pride. He couldn't imagine the actor *wouldn't* order the IPC detonated if he merely beat him into submission.

One solid hit with a bionic arm to the back of the neck ought to do the job. Savage raised his wrist, activating a comms device. "Joe, cameras!" Dazzling white lights blinded Crane, helped little by the night vision. It took him a few moments to realize the lights were coming from the cameras themselves. The unseen man monitoring the combatants must have activated them.

With a resounding crack, a kick connected with his torso, denting the chest plate and sending him flying back. *Bugger*, he thought, getting back to his feet and trying to blink away the spots before his eyes. He shifted his stance so that his bionic arm covered his body.

He heard movement to his right and threw himself in the opposite direction. Savage crashed into the stage where he'd stood moments earlier.

Crane closed his eyes, concentrating on the sound of the actor's footsteps. His opponent took a few shuffling steps, then there was no sound. He ducked immediately, feeling Savage sail overhead. He was telegraphing again. Even better for Crane, his vision was returning.

As they traded blows up on the stage, he could feel himself slowing. Already, he was physically and mentally exhausted.

Looking up, he caught sight of Sergeant Miller. The officer must have won his fight and made his way into the theater proper. Judging by the way he was edging down the side of the auditorium, Miller was trying to outflank Savage.

Crane redoubled his efforts, trying to hold his attention. "C'mon, boy. Can't you do better than this?"

Savage kicked out and Crane let the blow connect with his shoulder. *That's it, you've got me on the ropes now, haven't you?*

He heard a vague clunking sound and saw the floor drop away an inch from his opponent's foot. Realization dawned on him. Miller had opened a trap door, but a fraction too early. *Don't turn around,* Crane implored internally. *Keep your eyes on me, hotshot.*

Savage, intent on pummeling Crane, hadn't noticed. Thinking quickly, he snatched up the closest camera by the tripod and swung it. Savage parried with his right and his claws sliced straight through the aluminum stand. But he didn't see Crane's snapping front kick until it connected. His arms shot out, grabbing the foot as he overbalanced.

As though in slow motion, Crane and Savage toppled down through the opening together.

The second they disappeared from view, Miller charged down the stairs to the area beneath the stage, pausing to grab the stanchion and an emergency flashlight from its charger. In the light, he picked out the suited combatants.

He had no idea how the hell Crane had managed to get ahold of his power suit, but it didn't look like it would be an issue for long. Their suits had taken the brunt of their landing, and neither suit looked in great shape. The legs of Crane's suit were mangled and the left arm of Savage's had come off.

The actor, trained in taking hard falls, had landed better and was already on his feet. He hauled a stunned Crane into a sitting position, then, keeping him in place with his left hand, drew back his right to strike at his neck with the claws.

Miller placed the flashlight on the floor and ran forward, hefting the stanchion.

As he closed in, he glimpsed his reflection in Crane's helmet, and Savage lashed out with a back kick. Pain exploded in Miller's midsection as he was hurled backward and landed hard.

He gasped. He could feel that at least two of his ribs were cracked. His vision blurred, though he could make out Savage staring at him.

"How the hell did you—" he began, then cut himself off. "Whatever. I'll deal with you next."

Miller said nothing, groaning in pain, but also with the effort of straining to reach inside his mackintosh. Savage walked back to Crane and tore off his helmet. Underneath, the older man looked paler than usual and somehow older. His face was drawn and his nose bled.

"How the mighty have fallen," Savage murmured. "You're a real pain, you know that? I haven't got any cameras down here. Now I gotta drag your broken ass back upstairs so I can broadcast the killing blow."

He knocked his opponent back to the ground, then bent down and grabbed his legs.

Meanwhile, Miller had managed to slide his Heckler & Koch UCP pistol from its holster. He hadn't used it until now, not wanting the noise to give him away. He took a deep breath in then released it as he pushed through the pain in his ribs, then raised the gun and leveled it at Savage.

He had five bullets and needed to make each one count. Savage turned around to pull Crane along behind him and stopped short. Miller pulled the trigger.

A thunderclap reverberated through the space.

Savage jolted. Either he'd been too dumbfounded at the sight of the ancient firearm or his altikinetic reflexes just weren't fast enough.

The bullet hit its mark. Miller fired three more times, staggering Savage, who dropped Crane. The actor gaped dumbly at the four holes which had drilled through his armor. Too late, he had now discovered that while his suit was many things, it was not bulletproof.

Miller watched him gingerly touch a claw to one of the holes and drew it back slick with his own blood. His expression was blank, as though his mind were ticking over, trying to comprehend what had happened. He groaned, clutching at his abdomen, and sank to his knees.

Miller let his arms drop to the floor. Behind Savage, he saw Crane rise to his feet and realized he'd been playing possum. He walked casually over and a bolt of fear shot through Miller. He tried lifting the gun again. Crane simply reached down and plucked the weapon from his shaking hands.

The sergeant glared up at him, daring the killer to shoot. Instead, he turned, and Miller could only watch helplessly as Crane advanced on Savage.

"You are finished, sir. Your suit is all that is keeping you upright," he said. "You're going into shock and will bleed to death within minutes." He circled predatorily around the actor. "I don't like you. Imposters are bad enough but incompetent ones are detestable. Granted, you put up a fight, but alas, your game is over. I'd be lying if I said I didn't take some personal gratification from this, but I shall make it quick."

Crane stopped behind him, clamping the bionic hand over his mouth and pressing the muzzle of the UCP against his temple. "One more thing to see you off into the afterlife, Chaddy. *Villas of Mars* was pretentious, overrated rubbish."

Savage didn't react. He just stared at Miller imploringly.

Crane dropped the gun and placed his other hand on the back of his neck. "Oh yes," he added. "*Your* performance was particularly shit."

Knowing what was coming, Miller closed his eyes as Crane gave a vicious twist. Letting the body fall to the floor, the serial killer picked up the UCP, strolled back to him and tucked it back in the holster. "There you are. Saved your bullet. Incidentally, good show, Sergeant. Damn fine shooting."

He didn't know how to respond, even if he had the breath to do so. Crane assisted him in raising his arms above his head to help the air circulate. He took a few breaths as deep as he could handle, then Crane helped him to his feet.

"Now what?" he asked.

"We should probably see to that exploding cannon," Crane said.

Going slowly for Miller's sake, they climbed the stairs to the backstage area where they came face to face with mercenary Bob, still carrying his remote detonator. The man stared at the pair, then let the detonator drop to the ground.

Too exhausted for fear, Miller simply looked at the device resignedly.

CHAPTER 27

When nothing happened, Bob's expression changed from perplexed to alarmed, then to furious. Propping Miller against the wall, Crane strode toward the mercenary. Bob went for his blaster, but Crane reached him first, hitting him in the throat with his bionic hand and crushing his windpipe.

As the mercenary dropped, he returned to Miller. "Sorry about that, but I'm bloody fed up with Mars Group."

Miller decided he didn't care. "How come we aren't dead?"

"We figured the disarm code."

They turned to find Officer West beaming, though her sidearm was aimed at Crane. A sheepish-looking Agent Nichols was with her.

A bolt of fear surged through him. Would Crane attack her as well? He wasn't in much shape to fight, but he could probably get the Mutilator in a clinch until she could get away.

Instead, Crane simply released him and placed his hands behind his head. "I'll come quietly, officer."

Keeping her blaster trained on him, West helped Miller walk while Nichols trailed along behind.

"How'd you guess the code?"

"I realized it had to be something significant to Savage. Then I remembered he's nominated for an Apollo award, so I had Wyatt look up the date of the ceremony. It fit numerically and stroked his ego too." She gestured at Nichols. "Found him tied up in a janitor's closet."

Miller was impressed.

"Agent Webber is on her way with a tactical team to take care of the stragglers," West said. "She's even agreed not to lift the lockdown until we can get our esteemed guest back to his accommodation."

Collins and Conway met them outside. As soon as they saw Crane, they had their weapons trained on him.

"Miller," said Conway. "How the hell did he get his suit?"

"Savage got his hands on it somehow. Must have wanted a fair fight."

"We need to get that off him *now*."

"Not yet," said Crane. "I'm not finished."

"You said you didn't want any trouble," said Collins.

"Yes, after matters have been resolved."

Collins readied himself to fight, but Miller intervened. "Seven-Three-Lima-Charlie, deactivate!"

Immediately, the suit locked up and shut down. Without power, it became too cumbersome for him to move in. "What on earth…"

"Vocal override," said Miller. "I met Lin Changi at that party the other night; the lady responsible for creating your suit. She was kind enough to share the safeguards she'd had her technicians install in case the prototype was ever stolen before it could be sold." Truthfully, he hadn't been sure if it would work, but it certainly had.

Crane smiled. "Very well played, Sergeant."

"Whatever."

Webber and her team arrived, joining Collins in covering Crane, while Conway and Wyatt dismantled the remnants of the armor and the bionic forearm, restraining him once again.

Nichols wandered over to the SUV and sat on the bonnet, staring vacantly ahead.

"Sergeant Miller, Officer West, Mr. Collins. Thank you all so much for your assistance in rescuing Agent Nichols," said Special Agent Webber. "And, of course, preventing a detonation that would have leveled downtown Baltimore."

Miller shrugged. "Just doing our job."

"Aren't we all?" Webber said with a wry smile. "Mr. Wyatt, if you could come with me, please, we could use a hand dismantling the IPC."

"See you guys back at the station," Wyatt said to the others, before following the fed and her team back into the Hippodrome.

"Alright, let's take Mr. Crane home," said Conway.

Conway lead the Mutilator into the containment van and magnetized the railing, which his restraints stuck to with a dull clunk. Miller and Nelson piled in after them, while Collins stood guard with his electroshock shotgun.

As Officer West started up the engine, Clarke jogged up, rifle slung over his back, and jumped into the passenger seat.

"Hey, Sarge, Baltimore VA Medical isn't far off," West called back to him. "We'll drop you off, get your ribs seen to."

Everybody in the back sat in silence, warily eying Crane. As the van turned into West Baltimore Street, there was an ear-splitting crash, the vehicle slid sideways and the world shook.

———•———

Crane was the first to recover. Having expected the collision, he'd braced himself with seconds to spare. The police were not so lucky. Most of them were unconscious or in the hazy limbo between states of consciousness. Either way, he had no more than thirty seconds to escape. A shame to leave without his suit, but time was not on his side.

Standing, he kicked out, smashing the glass over the emergency release button, demagnetizing the railing his restraints were stuck to as the back doors fell off their magnetic hinges.

He saw Conway, out cold, and noticed a small remote-like device by her foot. Bending down, he picked it up then removed and pocketed the power cell inside. It could come in handy. After a quick look to see that Miller wasn't seriously injured, he climbed over him toward the door.

Somebody grabbed his ankle. Looking down, he saw Officer Nelson, trying to focus his eyes and fumbling with his sidearm. Ordinarily, Crane would admire the effort, but his window of opportunity was fast closing and he lashed out. His foot connected, driving the young officer's head and neck back with a dull snap.

He regretted having to kill someone without knowing if they deserved it, but he couldn't let anybody get in his way.

As he jumped from the back of the van, he slipped off the restraints. Circling around, he spotted the armored Humvee which had collided with the van.

As agreed, the passenger window was down. Crane reached through, taking a shirt from the seat, swapping it for the top of his prison uniform and slipping the brown corduroy trousers over the pants. The cotton shoes would have to stay. As an afterthought, he leaned over and took the trucker cap from the unconscious driver, pulling it down to hide his distinctive baldness.

Suitably disguised, he set off up the empty street at a brisk walk, knowing running would look suspicious to any patrol car heading to the Hippodrome.

———•———

Miller jolted awake, pushing aside the pounding in his head, and analyzed the situation in moments. Cooke groaned and rubbed at her head, and Officer Nelson had an obviously broken neck. Miller would have to come to terms with that later. More alarming was that Crane and Collins were nowhere to be seen.

Despite the dull ache of his ribs, he hauled himself out of the van, drawing his UCP. He looked into the vehicle which had crashed into them. Slumped over the steering wheel was Stephen Singleton.

Clarke sat in the front of the van, tending to a head wound West had sustained. "Collins took off through the park. Go. I'll look after her."

Miller's injuries limited him to a loping jog, but he didn't have far to go and soon caught up to a limping Collins, who'd sprained his ankle in the collision. His electroshock shotgun looked badly damaged, but he clutched it like a life preserver.

"He went down there." He indicated a man strolling along the footpath through the middle of University Square Park.

Miller leveled his pistol at the retreating back. "Freeze, Crane!"

Surprisingly, he did, slowly turning around, arms raised.

"What are you doing?" growled Collins. "Just shoot him!"

Miller wanted to, but his aim was shaky, and with only one shot left, he didn't want to risk missing. He needed to get closer.

"You shouldn't have done this. I don't care what friends you have, I'll make sure you get the needle this time, even if I have to drive you down to North Carolina and inject you myself!"

"If I don't wring your neck first," added Collins.

"I'm sorry you feel that way, chaps," Crane said calmly. "Looks like this is checkmate."

Quickly checking the safety was off, he was about to squeeze the trigger when Collins made a choking sound. Miller looked over to see him fall, body convulsing. "Collins!"

The man was having some kind of seizure before his eyes. He turned back to see Crane vanish around the corner.

Knowing he was in no shape to give chase, he decided to stay with Collins. Deep down, he felt it was what Marion would want him to do, even though the man had almost killed him back in DC.

Miller tried to recall what he'd been taught when dealing with a seizure. All he could remember was that holding Collins down would only result in further injury. The hospital was about two hundred feet away. He forced himself to half-jog toward the medical facility, shouting for help as he went.

By the time he returned with a pair of nurses, an orderly and a guard from the ER, Collins had stopped breathing.

●————————————●

A few hours later, Miller sat in a hospital bed, waiting to be x-rayed. All in all, he'd been lucky. Despite the best efforts of the medical staff, Ezecki Collins could not be revived.

But Phineas Crane was still on the loose. He could be hiding in any number of places around Westside. As he'd been lying there, however, he remembered the microcapsules Conway was supposed to have injected into the Mutilator. During all the fighting with Savage and Mars Group, he had forgotten about them.

He'd called Captain Donovan, who rounded up a strike-team and sent them to Charles Center One.

Upon arriving, Officer Clarke reported that Allondra Conway had already activated a signal. While half the team stayed behind to keep an eye on the staff until backup could arrive, Clarke and West led the others to find Crane. Wyatt traced the signal to some sort of safe house not far from where Crane had made his escape.

Once again, Miller could only watch from a live-feed as the junior officers breached the flat.

They found the body almost right away.

Phineas Crane was slumped over a table, his right hand in a bowl. A single power cell lay on the table next to him.

"What is it?" one of the other officers asked.

Clarke kept his pulse rifle trained on the body as West took a closer look at the bowl.

"Geez, I think it's acid! He must have been trying to burn his fingerprints off."

That didn't surprise Miller. It seemed like the sort of thing Crane would do.

"Is he dead?" the other officer asked.

West placed her hand on the back of his neck. *"I'm getting nothing,"* she said. *"Not even a flash."* She felt for a pulse, then shook her head.

"Alright, people, let's wrap it up here," said Clarke, then turned to address the bodycam filming the operation. *"If you're watching, Sarge, you can rest easy now. It's over."*

Miller sighed with relief. As he switched off the live feed, he thought over what he'd just witnessed. It didn't feel quite real. For years, the specter of the Metro Mutilator had hung over his head and those of the BMPD as a whole. And now, after the death of so many officers, it was finished.

He knew he should be grateful for no further loss of life, but it was anticlimactic. No final showdown, no last matching of wits, no fanfare. Phineas Crane had slipped the mortal coil quickly and quietly, if not painlessly. He might have proven his superiority over Chad Savage and escaped the police at the Hippodrome, but for all his planning and guile, it was Conway who'd gotten the last laugh.

A knocking at the door broke through his thoughts. A nurse walked in.

"Alright, Sergeant Miller, we're ready for you."

He nodded and lay back. Exhaustion had hit him like a sledgehammer.

Maybe he *should* look into taking time off.

CHAPTER 28

One Week Later

Miller and Wyatt sat in Donovan's office. With them were Special Agent Webber and Chief Hesseman.

"Where's Fiona?" Miller asked.

"Captain Donovan has elected to take a week of leave," Hesseman told him. "I'll be in charge of the day shift until she returns."

Good for her, Miller thought. If anybody needed a break, it was the captain. He was a little hurt she'd never mentioned it to him, but then again she was a grown woman and didn't owe him any explanation.

"Gentlemen," broke in Special Agent Webber. "Thank you once again for your cooperation in our investigation. And I'd like to thank you on behalf of Agent Nichols as well."

"How come he's not here too?" Miller asked.

"He's currently on a flight to Venezuela. After physical and psychological evaluations, Agent Nichols he's been cleared for active duty. He's decided, however, to resign from the bureau. He will be missed."

"How did Savage find him?"

"He said one of the mercenaries jumped him outside the party at the Butler Parks Center," Webber said. "We've rounded up the rest of Mars Group. They'll be doing time for second-degree murder of federal agents, among other charges. Mr. Wyatt, how did things go on your end?"

"I've shut down Savage's message boards," the tech reported. "Though you might want to post some official warning to our crowd of voyeurs."

"The Wraith suits?"

"Destroyed."

"And the IPCs?"

"Wyatt's stripped out the internal workings," said Chief Hesseman. "We were thinking of donating the shells to the Maryland Historical Society."

"Fine. And Mr. Singleton has given a full confession as to his involvement in Crane's escape."

Wyatt brought up the official reports, projecting them from his digital pad.

"This is what we've got so far. Figured I'd run it by you first."

Webber looked at the reports. "How did Mr. Collins die?"

"The coroner put it down to natural causes," Miller said.

"You were there, Sergeant. Is that what you think?"

"I think Crane had something to do with it, but I couldn't tell you what."

Webber nodded. "We'll leave it as is, then. Could you send me a copy?"

"Will do."

Miller sensed there was something else.

"Gentlemen," Webber said. "I'm sure I don't have to tell you that as this is a federal matter, you'll need to keep quiet about the particulars."

"Sure. Like we need the bureau up our ass too," Wyatt muttered.

"So how do we explain putting Westside under a total lockdown?" Miller asked.

"Officially, this was nothing more than an act of domestic terrorism perpetrated by a faction not worth naming and thwarted by a joint venture between the FBI and the BMPD."

"What about Savage? Aren't people going to notice a major movie star going missing?"

"We've taken care of that too. Officially, he was involved in a tragic car accident, traveling between Baltimore and Detroit."

The fed gathered up her equipment and headed to the door. "You have my personal gratitude, gentlemen. If you require federal resources in the future, I'm sure we'll be able to sort something out. Good day."

So Crane had been right. The FBI didn't want to acknowledge that their agents had been killed by an actor, of all people. Granted, one highly-trained in martial arts and with access to a dangerous power suit, but an actor nonetheless.

Miller decided he didn't care. It had no bearing on him anymore.

Miller sat in the domestic airport of Thurgood Marshall, staring idly as he waited for his redeye flight.

While he didn't regret his actions in the past few weeks, they didn't sit well with him. Arguably they'd been part of his job, but he hated that it'd come to that.

Conway, a warden of a corporately-owned prison facility—a civilian—injecting a biological time bomb into a living person deeply perturbed him, even if the man was a convicted serial killer. At least she had been arrested for her maltreatment of the prisoners in her care.

But it was more than that.

After thirty-five years with the BMPD, Miller figured it was finally time for him to take a break too. He'd applied for long service leave, which had been approved almost immediately.

A change of scenery was called for. He and Marion had always wanted to go back to New Orleans after their weekend honeymoon there. His flight was booked, his accommodation arranged and his suitcase was packed. He'd even arranged for Clarke and West to take turns going around to feed Spartacus II. He was looking forward to seeing the Big Easy again.

His phone buzzed. It was Donovan. He didn't think she'd be calling him while she was on leave, but was happy to hear from her. "Hey, Fiona."

"Thank goodness I caught you before you got on board. I wanted to say goodbye."

"Thanks. I'm looking forward to some time off. Glad you're getting some rest too."

"Not exactly. Got called out to Elkridge. Family stuff."

"Everything alright?"

"Yeah, just gonna be tied up for a few more days. Then back to the grind."

"You should take a few more days."

"Nah, you know how it goes, Myles. No rest for the wicked. I'll see you when you get back. You'd better take plenty of photos."

He chuckled. "I'll do my best, but I doubt I'll be doing much more than sleeping and fishing."

"Well, you enjoy that. Take care."

"You too, Fi."

Miller hung up and stifled a yawn. He was doing that a lot lately.

"One coffee, straight, black and piping hot."

Miller looked up to see his sister-in-law standing there with a coffee tray. Her chaperone hovered a few feet away.

"Hello, Jazz."

"Hi. How are you?"

"Been better."

"I hear that."

"How's the program going?"

"It's going. You know. One day at a time."

He nodded. "Nearly two weeks, right?"

"Yeah. They're reducing my hexothil next week, then I'll be going cold turkey."

"Glad to hear it. Have a seat."

Jazz sat next to him and handed over one of the cups of coffee. It was a Greasy McGee's and it really hit the spot.

"I haven't been sleeping much lately," she admitted.

"Withdrawals will do that."

"It's not just that. I've been thinking a lot about Marion and how if I'd made better decisions, I could have been a donor for her."

"It's in the past." If he was honest, however, there'd been times when he'd blamed his sister-in-law for that too. But he was learning to let it go. "We can't do anything about it now, and Marion wouldn't want us dwelling on it. We'll have to settle for forgiving ourselves."

"Easier said than done."

The two chatted as they drank.

After fifteen minutes, Jazz had to get back to the clinic. "You're coming back, right?"

"Three weeks. Someone's gotta clean up this town."

She laughed. "See you when you get back?"

"You'd better," he replied gruffly, though there was a smile on his face.

"Yes, officer." She smiled back.

Miller waved as she walked back to her chaperone.

He sat by himself, mulling over the events of the past couple of weeks until his flight was announced. Draining the last of his coffee, he stood and walked to his gate.

He sorely wished Marion was with him this time but taking his memories of her along would have to do.

I can't go on. I'll go on.

ACKNOWLEDGEMENTS

First of all, a big thank you to my parents for always supporting and encouraging me with my writing. My sisters too, although to a slightly lesser extent (because they didn't raise me.) A big thank you to Fitzy, Ingrid and Mel, for promising to buy hard copies. At least I know I'll sell a minimum of three copies, and yes, I promise I will autograph them!

Most importantly, a HUMUNGOUS thank you to the kick-arse women without whom this book wouldn't have been possible. Doris Hopper and Christine Morgan (who also did my author photo) for reading my short stories during our time working at the op-shop and for lighting the proverbial rocket under me to take the plunge and finally write my first full-length novel. To Alizah Pomery and Dee Heath for chauffeuring services in exchange for the odd cheeky chapter, and helping me realise that the "Cheese Kings" were far too ridiculous a concept for the tone I was going for!

Many thanks also to Margaret Bell for being my beta-reader (you really get me!) and Joanne Oliver for plot consultation, as well as Anne Casey (Invisible Ink Editing), Amanda Greenslade and Lynne Stringer for proof-reading and editing (PublishMyBookOnline) bringing some coherence to my mad ramblings! A super big thank you as well to Julia Lefik for the terrific cover design, so I wouldn't have to inevitably resort to clipart!

And finally, to you, the reader who made it to the end of this book. The young struggling creative types like me immensely appreciate you for buying this book, or at least reading it if you borrowed it. It was a labour of love and there will be more to come!

ABOUT THE AUTHOR

Nathaniel is a Brisbane-based actor, director and playwright. In addition to shows he's written and produced for the Brisbane Anywhere and Short + Sweet Festivals, he's a semi-frequent participant in the NYC Midnight Short Story and Short Screenplay contest.

Analog Cop is his first foray into novel-writing.

www.ingramcontent.com/pod-product-compliance
Lightning Source LLC
Chambersburg PA
CBHW070632170726
48291CB00003B/988